BEING GOLDIE
(IN A "JUST-RIGHT" WORLD)

MICHÈLE OLSON

Being Goldie
(In a "just-right" world)

A Mackinac Island Story
(Book Six)
Michèle Olson

More Books by Michèle Olson

Fiction:
Being Ethel (In a world that loves Lucy)
Being Dorothy (In a world longing for home)
Being Alice (In a world lost in the looking glass)
Being Wendy (In a world afraid to grow up)
Being Nancy (In a world lost in mystery)
(Can be read in order or as stand-alones)
Non-Fiction:
5 Easy Steps to a Happy Birthday!
A practical, funny guide to a Happy Birthday every single year

Being Goldie (In a "just-right" world)

A Mackinac Island Story

©2025 by Michèle Olson. All rights reserved.

No portion of this book may be reproduced, stored in a retrieval system, or transmitted in any form or by any means – electronic, mechanical, photocopy, recording, scanning, or other except for brief quotations in critical reviews or articles, without the prior written permission of the publisher.

Published by Lake Girl Publishing LLC, Green Bay, WI

www.LakeGirlPublishing.com

info@LakeGirlPublishing.com

Scripture quotations are taken from the Holy Bible, New International Version®, NIV®. Copyright © 1973, 1978, 1984 by Biblica, Inc.™ Used by permission of Zondervan. All rights reserved worldwide. www.zondervan.com

Scripture taken from *THE MESSAGE*. Copyright © 1993, 1994, 1995, 1996, 2000, 2001, 2002. Used by permission of NavPress Publishing Group.

Library of Congress Control Number: 2025902064

Publisher's Note: *Being Goldie (In a "just-right" world)* is a work of fiction. All incidents and dialogue, and all characters with the exception of any well-known historical figures, are products of the author's imagination and are not to be construed as real. Where real-life historical figures appear, the situations, incidents, and dialogues concerning those persons are entirely fictional and are not intended to depict actual events or to change the entirely fictional nature of the work. In all other respects, any resemblance to actual persons, living or dead, events, or locales is entirely coincidental.

No reflection is intended upon the staff and management of any similar businesses or institutions. Furthermore, this work takes place in 1984. Any laws or viewpoints mentioned herein are grounded in that time period.

ISBN 978-1-959178-04-0 (Paperback)

ISBN 978-1-959178-05-7 (eBook)

NO AI TRAINING: Without in any way limiting the author's (and publisher's) exclusive rights under copyright, any use of this publication to "train" generative artificial intelligence (AI) technologies to generate text is expressly prohibited. The author reserves all rights to license uses of this work for generative training and development of machine learning language models.

ACKNOWLEDGMENTS

Book Cover Design: Karen Kalbacher
Cover Painting of the Little Stone Church
and Various Cover Elements: Michèle Olson
Interior Layout: Raymond A. Olson II
Editor: Sarah Lamb
First Edition: 2025, printed in the USA

THINGS THAT PEOPLE DON'T PAY ATTENTION TO:

Pigeons, pencils, and the front and back matter in books.

Most people want to hop right into the story. Once you're done, come back and read the front and back matter because there's great information I want you to have. Thank you for reading my Mackinac Island stories. You make them shine!

To Marlene and Maxine, dear friends who always encourage and pray through every project. You mean the world to me!

To Pastor James, Pastor Jill and the entire CRE8 Church family—you make every Sunday night amazing. If you are in the Green Bay area on a Sunday evening, please join us. You are always welcome!
www.CRE8Church.com

To the over sixty adventure pals—Bob and Chris, Jon and Mel, and Jeff and Lisa. Hanging out is such a joy!

To my cousin Lori Ann and my friends since— childhood, Jan and Carol, I treasure our times together.

To my Lisa. To find a friend with a heart of gold in my golden years is a true blessing. Thank you for listening to every "scathingly brilliant idea."

To my family: my husband Ray, Ben and Cassie, Molly and Danny. I love being Gee Gee xxxooo to Jett and Jace. I love you all beyond words.

To you dear readers, all my love and gratitude.

To God be all the glory.

Lessons of the Marigold

To bloom vibrantly despite harsh conditions? The beauty of the marigold is its reminder to persevere through all circumstances. Often used as a plant to protect surrounding foliage, the marigold shows the importance of supporting those around us. Remember the unassuming elegance of the marigold.

CHAPTER ONE

EARLY SEPTEMBER 1984, MACKINAC ISLAND, MICHIGAN

*I*f you are expecting to hear all about Goldie Locks—don't worry. You are at the right place. The difference is—you're not going to hear it all from her. You'll get a better and probably more truthful story from me, her sister, *Gilda* Locks.

Right now, we are on a ferry heading to a little island in the Midwest called Mackinac Island. Have you heard of it? I had to look it up in an encyclopedia that Granny had in her enormous library. Speaking of Granny, you won't understand much about us at all unless I tell you about our granny. Ever see the movie, *Auntie Mame?* Well, if you didn't, Mame is this very wealthy, free-thinking, unconventional, impractical, often bohemian exuberant character. Granny is like her except with tinges of being very buttoned-up at a moment's notice and without the lovable traits. In the story, Mame is an aunt who raises her nephew while travelling around the world. Along the way they meet all types of eccentric characters. That's pretty close to how we've been raised.

Our granny is rich. If there was a word that was way more than rich, that's how rich she would be. Wealth doesn't even cut it. She started out kind of average, but from what we can gather, around the time we were born, our gramps invented some kind of new battery or something like that with patents that propelled them into money. Then, Gramps passed. Our mom passed around that time, too, right after we were born. That left us to be raised by Granny, who, according to her, knew how to invest and rake in the dough.

Our mom wasn't married when she had us. We have never been told much about our dad. In fact, it's a forbidden topic. We don't remember our mom. No one who knew her is allowed to talk about her. There's one picture of her on the mantle in the big sitting room. That's it. One picture. There's also only one picture of Gramps. Granny's minions have never told us anything. She pays her house staff very well, so they always follow her orders to a tee. Even now as adults, she keeps us on a very short leash.

Right about now, you're thinking we're pathetic. Why don't we just drop Granny and get on with our lives? Fair question. Here's the honest answer. Granny will cut us off from our monthly stipends if we don't do as she says. So, you're right. We are pathetic. In our defense, we tried a few times to do some things on our own. Turns out she still has ways to "get to us" and make us miserable. No one would hire us, not that I blame them. We have no real skills. We tried college for a while and took easy classes, but then we had the brilliant idea to party more than we studied. We got kicked out. Struggling isn't in our DNA. We stink at it. So, "boo-hoo for you" is also probably what you're thinking. Poor little rich girls.

Oh yes, we've thought of that. Marry someone rich. Get their money and be done with Granny. Do you know any handsome, rich guys in their mid-twenties who aren't married or aren't weirdos? Neither do we. Truth is, I'm easily overlooked. Did I mention Goldie and I are twins? Yup, twins. But you would never know by looking at us. It's quite common for blonde babies to be born bald. I was born bald. Bald as a billiard ball. But Goldie? Goldie was born with a full head of golden curls. Yes, I've seen the pictures. Perfect ringlets surrounding her perfect face with her cute turned-up nose. Me? Bald. Big nose. And when my hair did come in after more than a year, it was poker straight, very thin, and always called "chicken hair" by our various nannies.

Goldie is perfect. Perfect hair, perfect figure, perfect skin. While I suffered through the normal acne stage of puberty, Goldie didn't have one blemish. How is that possible? But I digress. When she walks in a room, heads turn. Too bad she has no acting skills and no interest in acting, because she has everything else you need to be a movie star. But she inherited the Lock family's predisposition to perfection. Everything has to be "just right," or she is not happy. Everything is *never* "just right." That's why no guy is good enough for her, even if he is rich. I've never actually been asked to marry someone, but she has. Many times. She strings them along and then drops them. She looks like the picture of my mom on Granny's mantle. I guess I must look more like my dad. He didn't make the mantle.

I'm average. I think I mentioned my nose is too big for my face. Don't get me started on my ears which are very hard to cover with thin, straight hair. I eat too much. It makes me feel better. I *would* like to live five minutes without feeling like the other shoe is going to drop at any moment. I know nothing good is in store. I've always been afraid to make the break from Granny without Goldie, and she won't do it.

"Ugh, this boat ride is taking too long. When do we dock? What are you scribbling about?" Goldie asks.

"Nothing. My thoughts," I say quickly closing my journal. She doesn't need to see any of this.

"Well, your handwriting is almost illegible. Remember that penmanship teacher we had, what was his name?" Goldie asks.

"Ironically, it was Mr. Paper, but he made us call him Monsieur Papier," I say.

"How could I forget? Yes, Monsieur Papier. 'Ze curls, girls, don't forget ze curls on your letters.' Was he even French? I think someone said he grew up in the Bronx," Goldie says. "So many tutors Granny threw at us, but so little of what they taught stuck. Don't get me started on algebra. So, what's up with this island? We better be staying at a nice place."

"It's called Grand Hotel. I read it has the world's largest front porch with white wicker rocking chairs. That sounds nice."

"Granny could at least have told us what we're supposed to be doing on this island," Goldie says crossing her arms. "I bet it's humid. I can't stand frizzy hair."

"It is fall in the Midwest. That should help with humidity. You should have my straight hair. All it will do is become like a limp noodle. I'm sure this is no different than the million other unknown destination trips she sends us on. As usual, we'll get our marching orders from Granny one step at a time. Get this. I overheard people talking as we were boarding that there are no cars on this island, only horses and bikes," I say secretly waiting to see her reaction.

"What? No cars? Is it like *Little House on the Prairie*? Are we going to be milking cows? Man, what I put up with to keep my money. Huh. I wonder what Granny has up her sleeve. Maybe we can figure out a way to have her committed. Then we wouldn't have to live like this. No cars? How does our luggage get to our hotel? If they think I'm carrying my own luggage; they have another thought coming!"

Yup. The reaction I expected.

"Oh, wait, I see. Look," Goldie says pointing to a group of men near where we are docking. "They're putting suitcases in their baskets on their bikes. And there's a carriage that looks like it's out of Cinderella that says Grand Hotel on the side. Now, that's more like it."

Stepping off the ferry, all I can think about is what this hotel will be like. This Grand Hotel better live up to its name in the area of nice beds, chairs, and food. Heaven help them if they have to deal with Goldie Lock when things aren't "just right."

CHAPTER TWO

"Look at that guy. I'm not usually attracted to redheads, but hubba hubba. He is an exception!" Goldie says gesturing to a very handsome redhead looking at geraniums that line the porch of Grand Hotel.

After settling in here, I've finally convinced Goldie to simply sit down on a wicker rocking chair on this beautiful porch and take it all in for a few minutes.

"Goldie. Shhhh, people will hear you," I say looking around and thankful there's no one near enough to really hear us.

"Oh, calm down. No one knows us. We are in the middle of nowhere and thank goodness that breakfast was amazing. They're lucky that the room is gorgeous. Those canopy beds and seeing that funny lighthouse across the water, I like it. If things weren't up to my standards, I would have marched right down to the desk and let them know I would not tolerate anything less than the best," Goldie says, twirling a curl as she often does when she gets on a soapbox about something. "I wonder who the redhead is?"

"Probably some kind of guy in charge of the flowers. I mean, I've never seen so many flowers surrounding a hotel.

Beautiful marigolds, I know what they are, the rest ...such a variety! I like how the porch has all geraniums. It seems to be their signature flower. Did you notice the geraniums on the napkins and the China at breakfast?" I ask.

"Now that you mention it, there is a very different ambiance. There's so many bold colors and patterns that I haven't seen other places. They must use a designer from New York. I don't think anyone in these parts could come up with this look."

"I'm impressed. This place doesn't have the sterile feel of so many of the hotels we've been dumped at," I say.

"Yes, Granny certainly does have a knack for shifting us around to get us out of her way, although don't you think it's weird that we are truly in the middle of nowhere. I mean it's always LA or New York, or Dallas even. This place? Whoever heard of it. I do like these white wicker rocking chairs. Very soothing. And even though this may be the world's longest porch, if that's true, it's still cozy. Yes, cozy is the perfect word for what it is. That red head is quite the eye candy. I can't take my eyes off him," Goldie says.

Goldie is incapable of sticking to one train of thought at a time. She's always been this way. Another Lock trait I'm thankful I didn't inherit.

"Let's just breathe in this fresh air and enjoy ourselves for a change. See that water out there? I picked up this brochure, and it says it's the Straits of Mackinac. It's where Lake Huron meets Lake Michigan. And look at that magnificent bridge. One of the longest suspension bridges in the world. People even died while making it. Construction began on May seventh, nineteen fifty-four, and the bridge opened to traffic on November first, nineteen fifty-seven. They have some great brochures down by the concierge area. You should—"

"Yeah, blah, blah, blah. I'd be interested in a brochure on the redhead. Tall and handsome. He obviously works out. Flower boy, huh? I wonder what that's about?" Goldie asks.

"It wouldn't hurt you to learn more about this area so you could appreciate where we are. Maybe Granny will expect us to know something whenever she finally lets us know why we are here. And while drooling over the redhead, did you notice that older guy towards the end of the porch? I feel like he's watching us. He was in the carriage we took up here to the Grand, and we were also close to him at breakfast. Every time I look at him, he looks away," I say.

"Good. You go after the older dude, and I'll go after the red head. You're an old soul anyway. You probably need an older man. While I like them young and gorgeous."

"So, if you met a young gorgeous guy and he was an idiot, you'd pick him over someone who was average and had a sparkling personality?" I ask hoping I don't already know the answer.

"Oh, yeah. Every time."

I did know the answer.

"Everyone's looks are going to fade but a wonderful personality is forever," I say.

Oh, please Goldie. Show me a glimmer of hope when it comes to how you think.

"That's why it's good we are rich. Plastic surgery! I'll probably start in a year or two. Do you think Jane Fonda and Dolly Parton look that way naturally? Puleeeze. Plastic surgery. In fact, if I don't snag that redhead over there, I might have to keep my eyes peeled for a plastic surgeon. That way I could have a handsome guy and free touch ups. I would know he would keep his appearance up, too. It's a win-win! And Granny did offer you some help with your nose, but no. You had to turn her down."

"I know my nose is large for my face. Believe me, every time I look in the mirror, I know it. And if I forget for one minute, there's always you or Granny to remind me."

"Getting it tweaked is always an option. Why not strive for perfection? I'm sure a good plastic surgeon would do wonders, and you would be thrilled with the results," she says holding up her fingers and framing my nose as if she can imagine what a surgeon could do.

"Could we make a pact never to talk about this again unless I bring it up? Would you do that for me?"

"Don't be so touchy. You know I only want the best for you. We women have to be perfect to make it in this man's world. That's what Granny says."

"Yes, and we both need to turn out like loving, warm, authentic Granny," I say.

"Okay. Point taken. And yes. I won't bring up your nose. But if you would do a little contouring with some dark makeup on the sides, that would help with the—"

"That counts as bringing it up."

"Fine. You're my sister, I love you, and I want you to be …"

"Perfect. You want me to be perfect like you, right?" I ask.

"Only as perfect as you can be. There's nothing wrong with that."

"I know that in your own Goldie way you mean that nicely. But no more nose talk. Agreed?"

"Well, it's going to be hard, but okay. I mean it's the rest of us that look at you…"

"Still doing it…"

"Alright! Icks-nay on the Ose-nay."

When she speaks in our childhood pig Latin language, I can hope I've finally gotten through.

"Seriously? You're pulling out that journal thing again? What's with you and all the writing lately? Are you thinking about becoming an author or something?" Goldie asks.

"No. I told you. I like to write down my thoughts. Maybe I can make some sense of this weird life we have," I say, making sure I don't open the book for her to see anything.

"You know what I thought about this morning when I was putting on my make up? Don't you love this new plum color on me? I think it makes my cheeks pop. I read about it in a magazine, and I talked Jeeves into running around to a bunch of different stores until he found it. Ah, I miss Jeeves. I wish Granny would have let us bring him on this trip," Goldie says.

"Jeeves is a human being, Goldie. Not a trained monkey to do your bidding. He likely got in trouble when Granny discovered he was running errands for you instead of taking care of things in our house," I say.

"Please. Call it what it is. A mansion. Don't be afraid to say the word mansion. House. Harrumph. As if. Eight bedrooms, four kitchens, and fifteen bathrooms can hardly be called a house," she says.

"Which proves my point. He has a lot to manage. Far more important things than getting you plum blush. You happen to have him wrapped around your finger, like most everyone," I say.

"Oh, dear sister. The color green doesn't become you. Hey, remember how much make up that one tutor wore? She was teaching us pottery, and we kept making those extremely crooked vases. There's a skill we've definitely used in life. And here's another thing I thought about. Did you ever realize that during our growing up years, Granny owned a circus somewhere? I found that out from Jeeves. I think in the winter when the circus was closed for certain months, she had those people come and be our tutors! Our education is from circus people!!" Goldie says with a laugh. "We were educated by clowns and acrobats!"

"That would explain a lot, and yeah, the sporadic way we had school, then didn't have school. And the random classes. I think you're right. She found out any skill they had and set them up to teach us for a month or two. Because then they did vanish. Poof! Like a circus act! Ugh, there's that guy again. He *is* staring," I say.

"He thinks you're pretty and probably mustering up the courage to come and introduce himself. Speaking of introducing yourself, I'm going to make my move. Mr. Redhead, time to meet Goldie Locks, your future girlfriend."

"Sit down girlie. Your future beau just kissed a certain little blonde on the lips, and now they're heading this way!"

CHAPTER THREE

"Are you sure it was on the lips, not the cheek or forehead? Maybe they're siblings, or cousins, or..." Goldie says, turning to see if she can convince herself I didn't see correctly.

"It was on the lips, and it lingered. Not siblings, and shhhhh, they are almost here," I say.

"Hi ladies! Isn't this a beautiful day?" the redhead asks.

"Are you enjoying your stay here on the island?" the blonde asks.

"Yes, it's lovely. We've never been in the Midwest much and never heard of Mackinac Island, so we are pleasantly surprised." I glance at Goldie who has a big pout on her face.

"I'm sorry, I should introduce myself. I'm Piper and this is my husband Cam," the blonde says extending her hand to me.

"Nice to meet you both," Cam says.

"Nice to meet you, too. I'm Gilda and this is my sister Goldie." I give Goldie's foot a little tap so she will snap out of it and act civil.

"Oh, it's my pleasure," Goldie says never taking her eyes off Cam and offering her hand to him like she's in some French movie waiting for him to kiss her hand.

"Goldie suits you with your curls. I bet you get called Goldilocks a lot," Cam says.

Now she's back into full flirtation mode. The girl can't help herself.

"I do, especially since Locks is our last name! But I'm Goldie with an 'e' at the end."

"Your name is Goldie Locks? And you're Gilda Locks? Are you twins?" Piper asks.

"We are," I say. "Fraternal of course, not identical, obviously."

"Oh, I see a big resemblance. Sisters. So lovely to meet you. We won't take up more of your time, but I wanted to give you one of the cards from my shop. I have a creative arts store downtown called The Creative Lilac. We have classes and carry a nice array of art supplies. I always like to spread the word to Grand guests who are interested in art," Piper says, handing me a card.

"And you, Cam, do you work in the store, too?" Goldie asks.

"I help out sometimes, but I have my hands full being the groundskeeper here at the Grand," he answers.

"So, we have you to thank for all these beautiful flowers we've seen on the island?" I ask.

"Me, and the wonderful Grand Hotel staff. I think we'll give the growing credit to God." He grins.

I want to smack her. She's touching his arm and giggling way too much. If I were Piper, I'd deck her.

"We must be on our way, but Gilda and Goldie, if you need anything from The Creative Lilac, my number is on the card. We also deliver supplies if you like to paint here on the grounds. Many people become porch-painters while visiting," Piper says.

"Are you staying for more than a few days?" Cam asks.

"Oh, yes. For...well, we don't know how long but longer than a few days." Goldie flashes him her signature fully dimpled smile.

"I do love art—some mixed media, but my favorite is watercolor," I say.

"Bingo. That's Piper's specialty. She paints the Round Island Lighthouse you see out there, the flowers, the Grand, and many of the island's main scenic sights," Cam says moving closer to Piper and putting his arm around her.

He clearly is in love with her and hasn't reacted at all to Goldie. Thank goodness.

"I love painting these amazing island scenes, and people seem to enjoy taking the paintings as souvenirs of their time here. That's one of the classes I teach—how to paint island sights. I hope you can make it to a class," Piper says.

What a nice lady. They seem to be in their early thirties, not that I'm a good judge of age. People think I'm thirty and Goldie is twenty. Twenty-two, I have to tell them. Twenty-two-year-old young women who still have to do whatever their granny says. I don't know if it's this fresh Upper Peninsula Michigan air or the fact I've started writing things down, but I've never felt more discontent with how we are living our lives. Maybe I can convince Goldie we can do better on this trip.

"I will check it out, for sure. Are you open normal business hours?" I ask seeing Goldie move closer to Cam.

"Actually, the hours are on the card. See there?" She points to the back.

"Oh, good. I'll plan a walk down to the town, soon. Thanks again, and sorry to be on our way, but my sister and I have an appointment," I say gathering up my bag and grabbing her arm while pulling her forward.

"We do?" Goldie asks, fighting my pull.

"We do. You know that thing. Great to meet you Piper and Cam. Bye," I say, moving us both forward.

"Bye. Bye, Cam. I'll see you around the porch again, I hope. Oh, and nice to meet you too, Piper." Goldie says as we head for the parlor that leads to the elevator. "What's the big rush Gilda? I finally got to meet him."

"Press three," I say as we enter the elevator. "I wanted you to show me that new blush you got. Maybe I will use it," I say mustering every ounce of self-control to sound normal.

"Oh, good! You know at first, I was mad that Granny didn't let us have our own rooms, but now it's kind of fun to share a room. I mean especially if you're going to let me show you my makeup techniques. The plum wasn't the only color in which I was interested. Here's our room. They had the shiniest shade of peach that would…"

I enter our room after Goldie and shut the door.

"Shut up!"

"Gilda! What did you say to me?"

"Shut up! I didn't bring you up here to talk about stupid make-up. I would like to kill you for embarrassing us so much. Cam is married and you stood right in front of his wife and touched his arm and flirted. What is wrong with you?" I'm so mad I'm spitting when I speak.

"You're mad about that? A little harmless flirtation. All people do it. Besides, it was a test. What if their marriage was on the rocks and there was a possibility I could get to know him? You never know," she says, sitting down in front of the vanity and applying more blush.

"There are boundaries in life, Goldie. You don't flirt with married men on the basis their marriage might be in trouble. I need you to see that what you did was wrong," I say.

"Fine. I didn't know I had another guard dog besides Granny. Now you are taking on that role, too?"

"There's an enormous difference between me and Granny, and you know it. Granny does what she does…well…I don't even know why she is the way she is. But I'm your sister. I want only the best for you. You're the most important person in the world to me. I hope we can break from Granny and find our own paths," I say. "We can't go on living lives that satisfy her whims without any regard to what we should be doing for ourselves."

"Please. Not the 'give up the money speech' again. I won't. I'm not going to take some low paying job I hate for the rest of my life, and I'm not going to marry a slob and have him run my life because he has money. I won't do it," she says stamping her foot for emphasis.

"Those aren't the only two options. We could get decent jobs and help each other. Imagine living where we want. Doing what we want."

"Imagine having to worry about the price of bread or clothes or make-up even. Imagine we don't have enough money for rent, and we live in a seedy part of town where we are afraid to walk home at night from our low paying job. And when we don't have enough money, we have no one to turn to. Granny is our only option. Say we leave and fail. Then we come crawling back. What's next? Even more stipulations about how we live our lives. You aren't being realistic. Okay. I get it. I shouldn't have flirted with Cam once I found out he was married, but you aren't the moral police. We are twins, but I have the right to live my own life. I have my fill of boundaries from Granny!"

I'm a little surprised to hear she has given serious thought about leaving Granny's grip.

"Goldie, I don't want to fight. I don't. Piper seems nice. I was embarrassed. Hopefully, they didn't see it as flirting. Just promise me you won't pursue Cam in any way. I'm sure there are plenty of nice young men to meet while we're here. Lay off Cam."

"I wasn't going to pursue him, I was just making polite chit-chat," she says.

We both know that isn't true.

"Can we be done with this topic now, please? I do want to try this blush on you. You owe me after telling me you'd like to kill me," she says with a smirk.

"Not literally. And yes. That was harsh. I'm sorry. Okay, you can try the blush on me," I say moving toward the seat on the vanity.

"Oh, goodie. Now wait until you see how color can make you pop…"

Knock, knock.

"Ugh. Who is that? We don't know anyone here—" Goldie says.

"I don't know. Did you order extra towels or something?"

As I open the door, I see one of the hotel workers.

"Good afternoon milady. Are you Miss Lock?" he asks.

"Yes, I'm Gilda Lock."

"This telegram arrived for you."

"Oh, thank you. Let me get you a tip…"

"No, milady. No tipping at the Grand Hotel. It was my pleasure to serve you."

This place is different from all the hotels we've been to. Usually, hands were always out awaiting a tip.

"Well, guess what. We just got a telegram," I say closing the door.

Yes, it's 1984 and no one else we know gets telegrams. We are used to it.

"Granny?" Goldie asks.

"Exactly. Granny."

CHAPTER FOUR

"I bet she's sending us to another island. What if we were supposed to go to Martha's Vineyard and somehow it was goofed up? I mean, has anyone ever heard of this place?" Goldie says while applying even more blush.

"Here goes," I say opening the telegram.

Hope you are enjoying your stay on Mackinac Island. Stop. It should be a lovely place for you to spend the fall. Stop. Let me know if you see any suspicious people. Stop. Behave yourself girls. Stop. I've arranged for you to meet up with an acquaintance of mine on the island. Stop. Her name is Katherine Sims-Dubois. Stop. Expect an invitation from her soon for high tea. Stop. Fondly, Granny. Stop.

After reading it aloud to Goldie, my knees feel weak. I have to sit.

"Did you read between the lines? We aren't here for a week. We are here for the fall," I say.

"Yeah, I noticed that. Why? She didn't even give us a reason. And how are we supposed to know if someone is suspicious? We don't know anyone; everyone looks suspicious to me. Well, except for a certain—"

"Stop! You agreed."

"Fine. Oh, he's just so good looking. And did you notice his muscles? And red hair, it's so exotic."

"Goldie, I'll get a telegram to Granny right now saying there are all kinds of suspicious people here, and we need to leave right away if you don't stick to your promise," I say, giving her my look that means I am serious.

I know she's my twin sister, but at times I feel more like her mother than her sister.

"Why does Granny know someone on the island? A…what was her name…Katherine Sims-Dubois. We're getting an invite to high tea. I saw they have one every afternoon here at the Grand. There goes more of our freedom. She has someone to watch us and report back to her. So, like her. We can only hope she's a sweet old lady who will have tea and then leave us alone," I say.

"You're going to think I'm crazy for saying this, but it's been mulling around in my brain. I think I'm on to something. Do you want to hear it?" Goldie asks.

"With that kind of build-up, how could I resist?" I ask, then take a big drink of water.

"I think Granny is part of the mafia."

I can't help but spit the water out while feeling like I'm choking. What did she just say?

"Excellent spit-take. Just like in the movies. Glad you were facing the other way," Goldie says laughing while handing me a towel.

"You think *our* granny is a mafia person? Like da Godfaddher?" I ask doing my best Marlon Brando impersonation.

"Yes! I think she runs it in some way."

"What are you basing this on?" I ask.

"How can she keep up her millions with just a battery patent or whatever it is Gramps was supposed to have invented? Think of the kind of people who came to have meetings with her. They could have all been cast in the *Godfather* movies. The older we get, the more she ships us off somewhere. I think she's afraid we will catch on and start asking questions. Think about it. You'll see, I'm not crazy," Goldie says.

She has valid points.

"You think she is doing illegal things and running gambling rings or extorting money from businesses? Wouldn't she be in jail by now?" I ask.

"Not if she's good at what she does. We are her grandchildren, and we don't know a thing about her. She's good at keeping things secret. And now I'm wondering about that guy you saw on the porch; the older one you thought was looking at us. What if he's one of her hench men she sent here to watch us?"

"That thought gives me a headache. I think we're being paranoid. I want to have fun and relax. Why can't we have a normal life?" I ask.

"Ha! You were born into the wrong family."

"You're right. Fun and relaxation is not Granny's modus operandi. She always has something up her sleeve. Once again, we wait for the other shoe to drop. And now we are on the radar of one Katherine Sims-Dubois. The shoe! I see it slowly falling from the sky," I say, draping over dramatically to get the giggle I wanted from Goldie.

"Anyway. Think about mafia Granny. You'll see I'm right. I know what we need—two words." Goldie says with a big smile.

"I know those two words. You're thinking retail therapy," I say.

"Now you're talking! Let's go Woo-hoo. Retail therapy is my favorite. I was about to go through shopping withdrawal. I haven't bought anything new for a week."

"Um, there's a bag over there with something in it from one of the shops on the ground floor right here at the Grand," I say.

"Oh yeah, I did get some stuff there. But it's little stuff. A scarf and a bracelet, nothing big. I love buying stuff. See? That's another reason we don't poke the granny bear. She keeps our bank account full if we do what she says. We can buy so many pretty things!"

Gosh, I hope she's kidding me. Somehow, I must get her to see what's important in life beyond having more stuff. She needs to understand we need to be on our own and figure life out for ourselves. We need to grow up!

"Give me a minute to freshen up. I'll meet you down in the parlor," I say.

"They should have some really cute islandy clothes, at least I'm hoping they do," she says heading out the door. "See you soon."

After throwing my hair up in a ponytail and taking *off* some blush, I head for the elevator. I might as well enjoy each moment on this beautiful island. Taking the elevator down to meet my sister, I'm not sure if I should laugh or cry. Our granny, a mafia big wig. Still, I have seen seedy characters come through our doors. What if Granny *is* involved with illegal activities? What would that mean for Goldie and my future? Could we be seen as part of it and be in trouble, too? Did she send us here to hide us from some big thing going down?

Oh, retail therapy is definitely needed. Downtown Mackinac Island here we come.

CHAPTER FIVE

"I saw the guy again," Goldie says as I approach her in the parlor.

"The guy from the porch?" I ask.

"Yeah. He was talking to the concierge."

"Well, that's not a crime. I mean, he's a guest here. We're going to see him around," I say. "Did he look at you or do anything suspicious?"

"No, I guess not. And that's odd. Why wasn't he looking at me? Everyone looks at me."

"Goldie, you must have to wear only blouses with buttons, because I don't think you could get a pullover over your big head!"

"You know it's true. I can't help it. I make sure I always look good. *You* could use more blush. I thought we had that fixed," she says looking around to see if people are looking at her.

"Spend a little more time working on what's on the inside, not just the outside."

"You only have one chance to make a good first impression. I don't know who said that, but I heartily agree," she says fluffing her perfect curls. "And because you were so grouchy with me earlier, I looked at the brochures you talked about, and

I found out more about how this place is decorated," Goldie says.

"Well, good. That shows initiative…"

I want to say and "bravo for an interest in something other than yourself," but I don't.

"Tell me what you learned," I say.

"Just a few years ago, a certain Carlton Varney, an interior designer famous for his use of color in hotels, castles, and palaces…a guy with my kind of love for grand places I might add…and part of the notable Dorothy Draper & Company… again, right up my alley…"

It's amazing how she can retain things she is interested in while she can't remember the name of the gardener at Granny's who she has known her whole life.

"He's an author, an artist, and a TV personality. He has done designing for presidents and first ladies. It's his touch on this place that makes it sing. He's still working on designing. The brochure said there's three hundred and ninety-six rooms plus the rest of it, so that's going to take time. Did you know there's a Presidential Suite? It was one of his first projects. It's on the first floor and takes up three rooms. We should bug Granny to get us that one."

"Oh, because we're presidents or in politics at all?"

"No, because we're probably richer than most presidents."

"Granny is richer, not us. We still get an allowance."

"Anyhoo, I talked to the concierge and right now he's working on the Eisenhower Suite. And the inside scoop is that Mamie, Dwight's wife, loved floral prints and pink…so the walls are pink. I would love that! Maybe it will be done in time for us to get *that* room!"

"We are fine where we are. Be careful, or we'll get a bigger room and less money for retail therapy."

"Good point. Oh, I also found out Carlton was Joan Crawford's decorator, and he even met Bette Davis, can you imagine? You know those stars in all the old movies we see Granny and

Jeeves watching sometimes. Oh, the glamour! Well, I must say I love what I'm seeing around here even more after getting all this Carlton Varney knowledge."

"Maybe you should study design or architecture or something like that? I think you could be good at it," I say hoping to spark something in her to pursue a normal life.

"I can see it now, writing for *Better Homes and Gardens*. The famous Lock girls are enjoying their stay at the elegant Grand Hotel on Mackinac Island," she says using a brochure as a microphone on her pretend TV show. "Could I describe their bedroom designed by Carlton Varney? Why, yes. Yes, I could. Their lovely bedspreads are covered in large multi-colored pink and red roses encased in emerald green. Behind each bed is a complimentary draping in a lovely aqua curtain, falling from a sconce in the shape of a princess crown."

Somewhere in this monologue she has switched to a British accent.

"Falling from this crown outside the lovely aqua is more fabric of roses that perfectly match the bed \spread. Big stripes of pink and white cover the two elegant chairs, next to the large blue and white striped tablecloth covering the divine tiny table that sits in front of the majestic patio doors which lead to a balcony—a true tourist delight. Dark green lush carpeting finishes off this room which also has a small but adequate vanity where two gorgeous young women perfectly apply blush before meeting their handsome dates for an evening of dancing under the moonlight on the world's largest porch," Goldie says while bowing.

"Oh my gosh," I say laughing. "You did an excellent job of describing our room. You should write for a magazine or do a TV show. You would be great!"

"Thank you," Goldie says in her British accent before reverting to her normal voice. "Now, let's get going. I need to shop. Let's catch that Cinderella carriage and head down to Main Street."

"It's not far, let's walk."

"No, we'll be doing enough walking into each of those cute little shops," she says stomping a foot.

"I need some real exercise. You take the carriage, and I'll walk. How about we each explore the town in the way that sounds the most enjoyable? I'll meet you back in the room in time to get ready for dinner tonight. How does that sound?" I ask, hoping she goes for it. I could use a Goldie break.

"Yes. I think you're right. Besides, I'll want to try on everything in the store, and you'll want me to hurry up, so I like your plan. See you back here for dinner," Goldie says stepping up into the carriage that has just arrived.

I blow her a kiss as she waves at me from the carriage. Okay, Main Street. Here I come. What a gorgeous island this is! The sun is sparkling on the water, and if I didn't know better, the Straights seem to be filled with glitter. What is up with the Round Island Lighthouse in the distance? I think I've read about ten or more tidbits placed here and there throughout the hotel in the last few days to try to understand more about this beautiful place. I want to get to the fort and see that along with the island sites like Arch Rock and British Landing. Who knew I really like history when I get to see it in person?

Goldie can check out the clothes. I can't wait to see the art supplies at The Creative Lilac. The card Piper gave me says the corner of Market and Main. I'll follow Main to that corner and see what I find. Maybe I can see Piper and apologize for how Goldie acted. I'm still embarrassed.

The town is hopping! Island visitors are stopping and looking in windows while new visitors arrive on ferries. Horses and bicycles are everywhere. I love the clip clop sound. I almost feel like I'm back in time before there were cars. And fudge! The sweet smell of chocolate and sugary treats waft through the air making my mouth water. There will be fudge in my future.

Oh, Goldie. How did we twins turn out so differently? Not looks, that's a given. Our thinking is so different. I'm sure she will hit every clothing and jewelry store while I'll be looking for paper goods and island confections. I wonder if they switched babies at the hospital somehow when we were born She looks like the Locks. I don't. At least not any Locks that I know. What would my last name be if our mom had married our dad? I know there are ways to find out things these days, but Granny always made it perfectly clear any attempt to dig into our past would lead to her disowning us instantly. I could live with that, but she also made it clear, she would disown both of us, even if one of us didn't have anything to do with it. That directive wasn't by accident. She knows she can manipulate Goldie, but I'm more trouble. I couldn't do that to my sister. Even with her flaws, I love her dearly. She feels like the only true family I've ever had.

This is it! The corner of Main and Market and what an adorable sign. The Creative Lilac with lilacs in the window. The tinkle tinkle of the little bell as I enter makes me smile. This is going to be my favorite place to shop. I can tell already.

"Hello, Miss. Welcome to The Creative Lilac. Let me know if I can help you find anything," an elderly gentleman says behind the counter.

This is disappointing. I was hoping Piper would be the first person I saw in the store.

"Hello. I'm here for art supplies, but I would like to look around, too," I say.

"You take your time. If you have any questions, I'm here to help. My name is Freddy."

"Thank you, Freddy."

Looking around I'm thrilled. She carries the name brand paper and paints that are my favorites. Oh, and look. These must be her artwork. I love how she did Round Island Lighthouse and Arch Rock. And horses! She makes each one's personality shine through with her technique.

"Did you paint these pictures?" I ask knowing full well they are Piper's paintings. He's a quirky old guy. Maybe he'll try to take the credit.

"Hee, hee. I wish I did, but no. The owner of the shop paints them, one Piper Penn. Aren't they wonderful? She's always painting something new and putting it in here for sale. The shoppers scoop them up as fast as she can paint them. Each one is one-of-a-kind. I'm amazed at how many different ways she can paint one lighthouse," Freddy says.

Coming over to where I am, he opens a cabinet door under where the paintings are and pulls out another.

"See this one? She just did this one. I was letting it have more drying time. Even after all these years, I think it's one of my favorites," he says putting it in my hand.

The size of a small postcard, I hold it and see the immense detail with every brick on the lighthouse and the moon shining on the water.

"Oh, wow. It's a night scene. It's amazing," I say turning to him.

"What's amazing?" I hear someone say and turn to see Piper coming down the stairs into the shop area.

"Pip! Someone is in love with your latest Round Island Lighthouse painting," Freddy says.

"I didn't realize you had that down here, yet, Freddy. It was a fun one to do," Piper says coming over to us.

"Hey, Gilda, right? You made it here. So nice to see you!" Piper says.

"Gilda? Like Gilda Radner on *Saturday Night Live*, right?" Freddys asks.

"Yes, I do hear that occasionally. But not as much as my sister gets comments on her name," I say.

"Gilda has a twin sister whose name is Goldie, and get this, their last name is Locks," Piper says turning to Freddy.

Freddy roars with laughter.

"You see, Gilda, this is making Freddy very happy because he lives for puns and riddles and jokes and finding out there is someone name Goldie Locks is making him happier than you can imagine. Am I right, Freddy?" Piper asks patting him on the back.

"I couldn't love it more!" Freddy says, still chortling.

"I mean no disrespect to your sister, it's just so perfect. And does she have blonde hair like you?" he asks.

"Oh, yes, but not straight like my hair. Very bouncy golden curls," I say.

More laughter. I'm not offended. It makes me smile to see someone so happy over something so little.

"See that sign over there by the cash register? I will tell you a joke or a pun for a donation of any amount. We are raising money for a mission in Africa that our dear friend Sister Mary-Margaret runs. We've raised over two hundred dollars," Freddy says with an expectant smile.

"And what Freddy isn't telling you is, we used to have a problem with Freddy telling every customer non-stop puns. So, we produced this plan. People are welcome to donate any amount to get him to tell you a pun or to *stop* him from telling a pun," Piper says with a big laugh. "This is how we got control of an uncontrollable problem we had for a while, and we are helping our dear friend's mission at the same time."

"Yes, isn't that genius? Pip came up with it, and now we are all happy," Freddy says.

"Oh, Freddy. How can I resist? Here, let me put a donation in your jar," I say walking over and dropping all the loose change in my pocket into the jar.

"Okay. Hit me with one of your best ones," I say. "I'm ready."

"Thank you, Miss Gilda! You're my first one today. Here goes. I don't understand why my calculator stopped working. It just doesn't add up."

The look on his face is priceless. Then he bursts out laughing again.

"That is clever, and I've never heard it. Good one, Freddy. It just doesn't add up. Now, I'm going to go in my purse, get another dollar and give it to you for your jar. That's because I can only manage one such brilliant performance today. But I'll be back in the future for more. How does that sound?" I ask.

"Perfect! More money for the mission," Freddy says taking the dollar and chuckling his way back to the checkout area.

"Thank you for making his day," Piper says quietly to me.

"He's a delight. Is he your uncle…or?"

"He's family even though we aren't blood related. I knew him when I lived in San Francisco. When I moved to the island, he came here to live with Cam and me. He helps so much in the shop and has his room upstairs next to my meeting room and studio," Piper says.

"How sweet. He's fun. Speaking of your husband, I wanted to express my sincere apologies for my sister's behavior on the porch at the Grand. I'm sorry to say she was eyeing him up before she knew he was married, and then she didn't act appropriately when she found out he was. She can be a handful when it comes to handsome men. I was very embarrassed," I say.

"Oh, don't give it a second thought. Here's the thing about Cam. He doesn't know how handsome he is. That sounds funny, but he is not like that. He's not flirtatious at all. He loves to talk to everyone, because he's simply interested in people. Sometimes, women take it the wrong way, that he's interested in them. I've tried to explain it to him, but he's that clueless," she says.

"Well, you may need to teach him to be more direct with people like my sister, like, back off. She doesn't read the room at all. But I am sorry. It was so nice of you both to introduce yourselves and tell us about the shop. I may never have found it because I'm not the shopper my sister is. But this is exactly what I need. In fact, I'd love to get this painting you did of Round Island Lighthouse. I also need some basic watercolor supplies. I think sitting on the porch of the Grand, looking at the beautiful surroundings would be a relaxing way to paint."

"Oh wonderful. Yes, that is a special one of the lighthouse.

I'd be happy to know that you were the one enjoying it. You're welcome to get the individual supplies you need, but I have put together a kit to make it easier with postcard size watercolor paper, a travel kit assortment of paint and various paintbrushes. I think it's everything you need to get started," she says pointing out a kit.

"That is perfect, I'll take that too. What a great idea," I say.

"And, every Wednesday evening, I do a class where we paint different island landmarks in my studio upstairs. You're welcome to take the class. You don't need to bring anything. I supply all the materials needed, and you take your finished piece home with you. Are you staying on the island long?"

"We're not sure, but after some recent news, I think it's going to be longer than we thought. So, I should be able to make that class. Is it every week?"

"Yes, every Wednesday evening at seven pm. We have a Bible study from five-thirty to six-thirty and then the class at seven for painting," she says.

"You study the Bible? Like, religious Bible?" I ask.

"Yes. It's so much fun. There's this wonderful group of ladies I know from church, and anyone is welcome," she says gathering up my kit and painting. "Have you ever read the Bible?"

"Um, no," I say.

What an odd question!

"Our granny who raised us always talked about religion as something people make up. We had one class on religions of the world, but that was about it. I was so bored I wanted to sleep through it," I say before realizing that may be offensive. "Oh, I'm sorry. I didn't mean to offend you."

"I love that you tell it like it was for you. But here's the thing. I'm all for someone telling me they don't believe what it says in the Bible *if* they've read it. But if they are basing their opinions on what others have said, and they haven't read it for themselves, that's when I speak up. I challenge people to read the

Bible, especially to start with the book of John. Then I'm happy to hear what you think about it."

"That's wise. I've never even held a Bible."

"Well, when I bag your purchases, I'm going to put in there a New Testament, a modern version Bible, so you will have one. Then you can say you've held a Bible. The fourth book in there is the book of John. That's where I suggest you begin to read it. Then, tell me what you think. It's that simple."

"Oh, you don't have to do that," I say hoping she doesn't.

"I know I don't have to, but I want you to have it. You'll see. At some point in your life, you'll be glad you have it. Maybe not right now, but sometime. It will come in very handy," she says with extreme confidence.

"And you don't mind if I skip the Bible class but come to the watercolor class?"

"Of course not. Some people come for one or the other, whatever they want. Each week is different, and that's how we like it."

"Is ze watercolor class open to anyone?"

The speaker's deep voice startles me. I've been so involved in what Piper was saying, I was oblivious to anything or anyone else in the store. Turning to the voice, my mouth drops. It's the man from the porch!

"Excuse me, Gilda, I have to help this gentleman for a moment, but wait if you can, I'd love to chat more," Piper says, heading for the man who seems like he's been watching us too much.

"Monsieur Chapeau, I'm so happy you were able to make it to the shop," Piper says to the gentleman.

"Bonjour Madame Piper, yes. I couldn't stop thinking about ze fact you mentioned an interesting product you had that would work better to spread my paints. The idea intrigued me because of what it's called, and how it is made, oui?" he says with a pleasant smile I hadn't noticed before.

I wasn't expecting him to have a French accent.

"Yes, when you were telling me how you wanted your watercolor to wash out more, I knew you were looking for ox gall liquid. It's a wetting agent that improves the paint flow," Piper adds.

"It literally comes from ze ox, no?" he asks.

"It's crazy, but yes and no. It comes from cows, specifically the gallstones taken from the cow's gallbladder. The gallstones are then refined with alcohol to create a watercolor surfactant," she says.

This is an interesting conversation. To think I was afraid of this man just moments ago.

"Surfa...surfa...I don't know this word. Si vous plait, explain?" he asks.

"Yes, please for me too," I say moving closer.

"A surfactant is when a chemical solution disrupts or disturbs the surface tension of another substance. As artists, we use it to disrupt the water. The molecules disperse within it. The effect is so cool, because you get a softer blend as the pigment disperses easier because of the increased flow of water."

"This is très amazing, no?" he asks.

"You do have to be incredibly careful and use no more than three to five drops. It's best to start with less. You can always use more as you get used to it. So, you add a small amount to your water. You either use it as an overall wash for wet-on-wet work or add it to your mixing water for wet-on-dry. Here, look at this piece," Piper says picking up a beautiful painting of Round Island Lighthouse on a bigger canvas than the one I have set aside.

I can't stand it. I must dive into this conversation.

"Can I see this closer?" I ask. "I don't mean to be eavesdropping, but I find your conversation fascinating for someone who merely plops watercolor on paper," I say, hoping I'm not being rude.

"Oh, not at all, Gilda. This is for all you artists who come into my shop. I want everyone to know all the cool techniques that are within the realm of watercolor and mixed media. And forgive me, I should have introduced you! Gilda, this is Monsieur Chapeau, a fellow artist I met while making my rounds on the Grand Hotel porch," Piper says, gesturing toward the gentlemen who suddenly doesn't look ominous at all.

I'd say he's in his early forties. The little graying in the temples of his black hair peeking out from the gray fedora matches his suit. He's definitely debonair.

"Seems appropriate you are wearing a hat Monsieur Chapeau with your name," I say, reaching out to shake his hand.

If he's an axe murderer sent by Granny or one of her henchmen, he might be less likely to hurt me if we are fellow artists with newly acquired ox gall liquid knowledge.

Shaking my hand, he bows slightly.

"You parlez-vous français? Mademoiselle?" he asks.

"Très peu, monsieur, which I think means 'very little' if I remember my French lessons," I say, nodding my head in return.

"Your accent is particularly good. And please ladies, you must call me Remi," he says.

"Since you are both such interested students, I also must tell you about gum arabic, which is the hardened sap of two kinds of acacia tree. The opposite of ox gall liquid, it's a binder for watercolors. It slightly increases the drying time, which gives you longer to manipulate blends and washes. I love how it adds a glossy finish to dried paint. See, on this piece, I used it to create more interest in the sunset because of the gloss it makes," Piper says, pointing to a painting.

Just like me, Remi is also tipping his head closer to see the painting.

"Yes, I do see," I say as Remi nods too.

"When you are putting it on it has a slight yellow tinge, but don't worry, it dries clear and doesn't change the color of the paint you are working with. I like this too. If you apply the gum arabic to a wet area of the paper, and then add other colors, you'll see the colors don't bloom out as they usually would. Instead, the effect is featherlike and much more gradual. So, when you want more control and a steadier flow in certain areas when you are working wet-on-wet, use gum arabic," Piper says.

"Piper, you are some kind of painting genius," I say.

"She's the best there is, that's for sure!" Freddy yells from across the room.

"It's lots of trial and error and study of what works and playing to see what all these things do. There is always something new to learn, and I do love it," Piper says.

"So, to get ze flow you need ox gall liquid and for more control or gloss, you need gum arabic," Remi says.

"Exactly. You get more depth in your technique, and they allow you to fine-tune your style. That's what is so interesting. I'll do a class on painting the Round Island Lighthouse, and everyone's finished painting looks different. Every person puts their unique personality into their work. My hardest job is not teaching painting. The hard part is getting my students from hindering themselves, because they spend so much time listening to their inner critic instead of just enjoying art for the sake of art," Piper says.

"If you can accomplish that, then you are a miracle worker," Remi says. "For me, it is ze hardest. I tend to be disgruntled if I perceive it is not perfect or as we would say-parfait."

"Ah, parfait means perfect in French. Here it's a frozen dessert. But I hear what you're saying. I like things to be perfect, but my sister is the worst. If things aren't always 'just right,' she can't handle it. It's always 'too this' or 'too that.' Oh, sorry. I should be talking about me, not my sister," I say.

"This is ze lady with you on ze porch? Ze girl with ze golden curls?" Remi asks.

"Yes. Everyone notices those curls. Her name is Goldie, and our last name is Locks. So...wait. Do you know Goldie Locks and the Three Bears where you are from? France, I assume?"

"Oh, my. Goldie and Gilda Locks. That is très jolie!" Remi says, chuckling.

"And they are twins!" Piper adds.

"Well, you are both beautiful young ladies. And, no, I am not from France. Somewhere closer to this beautiful island in fact. Can you guess where?" Remi asks.

"It has to be Quebec, Canada," I say.

"Yes. I am from Quebec. I have had many times in the States, but I was born and raised in Quebec."

"I didn't realize that! I assumed France, too," Piper says.

"It's quite common. People forget about our little French community to the north," Remi says with a twinkle in his eye.

Why was I so creeped out by this guy before? He seems like someone who would make a perfect uncle. Someone who would take you on trips to adventurous places and show you the world he knows. Remi Chapeau. It's a good name. Uncle Remi. I wish I had an Uncle Remi who loved to sit and watercolor with me.

"You guys have given me an excellent idea," Piper says. "I should do a class and demonstrate the ox gall and gum arabic… showing how they work differently. I was just thinking about what type of new and interesting class I could have next, and you two show up and give me the perfect idea. Thank you!" Piper says with a big smile.

She sure is a happy, easy person to be around. I wish Goldie would have come with me instead of spending time getting more clothes she doesn't need. Maybe I can talk her into coming another day.

The tinkle of the bell as you enter The Creative Lilac rings, and a gentleman in a black suit and black hat enters, nods to Remi, and quickly exits.

"This has been ze most exquisite time, but I must be going. I have some business to address. Piper, I am very interested in ze class you mentioned and Gilda, perhaps we can paint on ze porch of ze Grand together sometime? Piper, please put together whatever you think I need, and I will take advantage of your delivery service for the supplies. Here is one hundred dollars," Remi says taking a bill out of his wallet. "Please provide whatever this will get me for porch painting. If there is any change, please put it in your fundraiser jar I noticed by the register. I'm sorry to run, but business calls. Au revoir," he says with a tip of his hat as he rushes out the door to join the mysterious man.

"Wow, what a whirlwind," I say. "Do you know what he does for a business?"

"No idea. I only saw him alone on the porch, and we talked about art mostly. He sure is an intriguing fellow," Piper says.

"Thank you so much for what you showed us today, Piper. I never knew any of this, but I love the idea of learning new things. I'll settle with Freddy for supplies and your beautiful painting, and then I better find my sister. Most likely she bought everything in every clothing store on the island. I have to catch her before she hits ups the jewelry stores!"

"My pleasure. I'll make sure you are aware if I can pull that class together soon. Even if it's you, me, and Remi, it would be fun. Pay attention to the paintings you see; you may find those techniques in other pieces. I love looking for it," she says.

"I will. I feel like an art detective. Thanks again, Piper. I'm sure glad you introduced yourself on the porch. You should keep doing that. I don't know if I would have wandered around town to find your store otherwise," I say.

"Yes, sometimes I wonder if I'm being a pest, but through the years I've met the most intriguing people. So, thanks for that encouragement. It gives me just what I need to keep it up," she says.

Back on the street and wondering where to start to look for my sister, I can't stop thinking about Remi. I was so enjoying his company until that guy peeked his head in. He looked like he could be in a mafia movie. What are you, Remi? A good guy, a bad guy, or someone who is incredibly good at portraying a good guy? For some reason, I want to know the answer.

CHAPTER SIX

"Seriously? Didn't you learn anything about how to put on blush? Why aren't you using the stuff I found for you?" Goldie asks coming at me with her makeup brush in hand.

"Back off, sister. I'll use it for dinnertime, but it's too much for high tea. We don't have the same idea of what works when it comes to makeup," I say weaving in time to miss her brush.

"But if you contoured the nose…"

"That does it!" I say grabbing a pillow off the bed and landing a nice blow to her face. "No nose talk!"

"Okay! I forgot! I'm trying to be helpful. You're lucky we're leaving soon. I don't want to mess up my makeup, or I would be retaliating, and you would be going down! To be continued…"

"Nope. You said you wouldn't say nose, so every time you do, expect something to happen," I say, giggling.

"Seriously. There is some weird stuff happening. This Remi guy you told me about and now a telegram making us meet a lady. Why don't we blow off this high tea and do something fun?"

"I would love to, but we would just make bigger problems for ourselves. Here's what we do. We go to the tea; we smile and nod at this old lady and then get you-know-who off our backs. Otherwise, she'll sic someone else on us."

"Fine. Katherine Sims-Dubois. Ugh. I hate meeting new people who don't interest me. She'll probably bore us with stories from the olden days."

"Whatever happens, let's get there ahead of time, so we can pick where we want to sit. We'll eat our cucumber sandwiches, sip our tea, and get on with our lives," I say as we head down to the main parlor.

As the elevator doors close behind us on the main level, I start my perusal for where to sit.

"Goldie, how about the couch on the other side of the room…"

"Good to be punctual, ladies. Always good to be punctual."

Oh, my word. This lady standing in front of us is a sight to behold. Goldie's mouth dropped even further than mine. I better pull myself together and cover for both of us.

"You must be Katherine," I say.

A slight jab to the ribs should bring Goldie back to earth.

"Uh, yes, you must be…her," Goldie says finally closing her mouth.

"You would be correct, ladies. Katherine Sims-Dubois. Chairwoman of the Mackinac Island Town Board," she says.

I don't know why I feel like I should curtsey or something, like I'm meeting a queen. Although this fashion queen is stuck in the 1960s. Her heavily dyed black beehive hairdo looks like the pictures I found in old *Life* magazines in Granny's library. The fluffy skirt she's wearing swishes as she sways. Her extended hand waiting for a handshake boasts the longest red fingernails I have seen in a while. There is even a book on the tip of each toe of her high heels.

"Are those embroidered chairs on your skirt?" Goldie asks.

Oh my gosh Goldie. That's not polite.

"Why yes, thank you for noticing. It was another fashion brainstorm I had. As chairwoman, I thought it would be quite whimsical to have various chairs embroidered on this lovely skirt. Chairwoman, chairs...get it?" she asks.

"Oh. Now I get it. I can honestly say I've never seen anything like that in any part of the world I've traveled to," Goldie says.

Thankfully, Katherine doesn't know Goldie enough to realize that it is not a compliment.

"I knew it would be a hit. Jolly good. Well, let's do tea, ladies. Here. This couch over here is my reserved area when I'm having a meeting. As the one who basically keeps this town running, I am always given priority when I have an appointment," Katherine says. "I don't leave anything to chance."

For being someone who lives here, this lady speaks very differently. Like Katherine Hepburn in those old Hollywood movies. Very sophisticated, and very few pauses. She didn't put a "t" at the end of don't. And she said, "Jolly good." She's not British.

Sitting down on the couch, I'm surer than ever I want this to be as short as possible.

"Help yourself to the delicious Earl Gray tea and as always, the sumptuous sandwiches and pastries as only the Grand can make them. Don't miss the strawberries dipped in chocolate. You'll absolut'ly love them! I can't believe how good they are this late in the season. Now, I have a million questions," Katherine says, putting a cucumber sandwich and one strawberry on her plate.

She did it again! She skipped the "e" in absolutely and the "t" in can't. Get in the twentieth century lady!

"So do we, Katherine. At least a million questions," I say with a wink to Goldie but making sure Katherine doesn't see. "First, how do you know our granny?" I ask.

"The truth is, I don't know her. A friend of mine from my illustrious days at boarding school in England, the only time I've left my beloved island for any length of time mind you—knows her. She contacted me to tell me her friend, your granny, had requested that I meet you girls and see if I could be of any assistance while you are here," Katherine says taking the tiniest nibble I've ever seen someone take of a strawberry. I'm not sure any of the berry went into her mouth.

"Oh, that's kind of you, but we are doing well, thank you. We haven't had anything we couldn't manage so far. It's a lovely hotel, a lovely island, and we have been enjoying it very much," I say.

"Yes, well, since my acquaintance made it sound like you may be here for some amount of time, I wanted to make sure you know a few things to watch out for while you're here," she says taking another non-existent nibble, this time of her sandwich. This beehive, swishy skirt, weird sounding, red nailed, nibbler is quite strange.

"As I mentioned, nothing on this island happens without my knowledge, and frankly, my approval. Someone must be the defender of our little piece of paradise, and since Mr. Dubois went on beyond, that has been my role to play. For the most paht, we have wonderful people here, but there are a few I'll caution you about. For example, I have a somewhat distant relative I'm sad to say who you should avoid at all costs. You'll probably run into him, because he is an employee of the Grand, although why didn't they get rid of him years ago, I'll never understand. It's the one complaint I have of the place."

Ugh. Say part. Part! Not paht. Use the "R"!

"Well, yes, please tell us. We don't want any trouble," Goldie says.

"You can't miss him. He has the most flaming red hair I've ever seen on a man; well, except for his equally horrible brother who thankfully is in the big house and not on the island," she says tipping up her nose in disgust.

"You mean, Cam the groundskeeper?" I ask.

"Oh, no. Don't tell me you've already met him and his bossy wife Piper. Well, good. You know who to stay away from," Katherine says.

"Cam? Gorgeous Cam? He's one of the most handsome men I've ever met. Redheads are usually not my thing, but that guy—well he is something else." Goldie says.

Oh Goldie, look at me. My eyes are telling you to shut up!

"My sister is a bit silly when it comes to guys, so please excuse her. We met Cam and Piper here on the porch, and I've been to their store for art supplies," I say still trying to give Goldie the stare that means to 'watch what you are saying.'

"Goldie, you fancy Cam, do you? Well, maybe you should get to know him, so you could help him come around to my way of thinking. The two of them are the only holdouts of property on the island. My holding company and I own everything else. It's their stubborn, insensitive nature that prevents them from doing the right thing and selling it to me. I would rent it so they could have the store, but they insist on keeping it. They are so selfish and have been a thorn in my side ever since—"

Stopping abruptly, Katherine seems to realize she's lost control for a moment and said more than she wanted us to know.

"Well, who knows what the future holds. Goldie, you are just lovely with your curls and dimples. I bet you turn men's heads all the time!" Katherine says in a syrupy voice that makes my stomach churn. "You and Cam would be so cute together. Just between us, I think he and Piper are on the outs and haven't had a happy marriage for quite some time," she says.

"That's what I told my sister! You never know if someone's marriage may be almost over. See, Gilda, he may need a shoulder to cry on…" Goldie says.

"Stop Goldie. And Katherine, if you don't like these people, I highly doubt you know the state of their marriage or that they would confide in you. I spent time with Piper and from what I know, they are very happily married. My sister will not be doing anything to cause a rift between them. Really. I'm offended," I say.

It's taking every ounce of self-control not to pick up a sandwich and throw it in her face!

"Please lower your voice. You're causing a scene. I merely suggested there's no reason your dahling sister can't be with whomever she wants. It's a free country," Katherine says in a snit.

The word is darling, lady, not "dahling."

"Would you have liked it if women threw themselves at Mr. Dubois back in the day?" I ask.

"Mr. Dubois was married to me, so he had no reason to look at anyone else. Why the mere suggestion is preposterous!" Katherine says in a huff.

Her tone makes me think Mr. Dubois might have been a flirt.

"Thank you for inviting us to tea Katherine, but we have another appointment to keep. Rest assured we are fine, and you can convey to your friend, who can convey to our granny that we are doing well. If we need anything, we'll be in touch. Otherwise, you can go about your terribly busy schedule and not give us a second thought. Thanks again," I say rising and grabbing Goldie's arm mid tea sip, causing a little to drip on her shirt.

"Darn it, Gilda! I just got this!" Goldie says grabbing a napkin and dabbing the soon-to-be stain.

"Let's go!"

"Oh, Goldie, if you ever want to have a chat, please stop by my office on Main Street. I think we could be great friends. I have lots of ideas about how you could become a good chum to whomever suits your fancy. You're an adult after all. You can do whatever you want. Tah, ladies. Remember, it's my job to know what's happening on my island at all times."

"Katherine, what was the name of Granny's friend who contacted you?" I ask.

While Goldie is still dabbing and muttering under her

breath about my clumsiness, Katherine stands and starts walking, swishing away with that ridiculous skirt with chairs on it, moving toward the doors leading out onto the porch. So, you don't want to answer my question, huh?

"Did you notice she had little chairs painted on the tips of her high heels? I mean, who does that? I say.

"Don't change the subject. Tea is hard to get out of a white shirt. And why did you get all grouchy with her? She was just trying to help us get to know the ins and outs of the island, for Pete's sake. Sometimes you are so insensitive," Goldie says turning back toward the elevator. "Now I have to go change."

Once we are inside the elevator, and thankfully alone, it's my turn to speak.

"Listen, missy. She's a horrible person. Cam and Piper are lovely people, and it was clear she saw an opportunity to use you to cause trouble for them. Didn't you hear her? She wants their land, and they won't sell it to her. You are a pawn in her eyes. She wants you to flirt with Cam, who she just said two minutes earlier you should avoid. She's a snake!" I say.

"Then why did Granny have someone she knows go to the trouble of contacting her to have lunch with us?" Goldie asks. "Did you get the person's name?"

"You were too busy with your blouse to hear me ask her the name, but she wouldn't answer me. Another strange thing. And as to why Granny had her contact us, you just answered your own question. Granny wanted this Katherine Sims-Dubois to be another set of eyes on us. Do you suddenly trust Granny?"

"Well, no."

"Then do the math. Anything Katherine thinks is a good idea isn't for our well-being. Granny's plans always benefit Granny. Katherine is like Granny. Get it? Katherine is just a swishy skirt Granny," I say.

"Oh, I suppose you're right. Listen, after I change, let's go get some real food. She made me so nervous I didn't really eat my cucumber sandwich," Goldie says as the elevator doors open.

"Bonjour, mademoiselles!"

"Monsieur Remi, bonjour," I say stepping off the elevator.

"I see we are on ze same floor. And this must be your sister, Goldie," Remi says.

"Yes, Goldie, this is Monsieur Chapeau," I say.

"Please call me Remi," he says taking her hand and shaking it politely.

"Nice to meet you, Remi," Goldie says. "My sister told me about the great time you had at The Creative Lilac."

"Yes, it was amazing. I have received ze art supplies and am excited to try them. Perhaps you would both join me for some painting on ze porch later? We have so many beautiful things to paint right in our view," he says.

"Oh, not me. Gilda is the artist in our family. But I do have something to ask you, Remi. Who was the mysterious stranger who came and spoke to you right before you left Piper's store? Is he someone you work with here on the island?" Goldie asks.

Quickly looking at his watch, he abruptly moves away from us and heads towards the stairs.

"Oh, I'm so sorry, mademoiselles, but I realized I am very late for an appointment. Please excuse me. Have a wonderful day," he says turning completely and hurrying away.

"Goldie, part of me wants to once again tell you to quit being so blunt with people, but now the other part is wondering why he didn't answer. Exactly how many people does Granny have watching us on this island, and why is she so concerned with anything we are doing so far from her?"

"Mafia. I'm telling you. Mafia."

"That doesn't explain anything about us. She can conduct her mafia just fine without us and keep us here to stay out of her business. Something else is going on. And something inside me, tells me we better figure it out sooner than later."

"Yeah, whatever," Goldie says, unlocking our door and heading to get a new blouse.

I wish I were as easy-going as she was and didn't let all this bother me. But it is. It definitely is.

CHAPTER SEVEN

"Wake up, wake up!" Goldie is screaming in my ear. "Huh? What time is it? What happened?" I can't believe I'm still sleeping, and she is awake. That never happens. "I guess I was extra tired. All the weird stuff lately made me have crazy dreams. Wait, you're dressed?"

"Yes! That's what I want to tell you. I got up and went to breakfast without you. And I met the most gorgeous man! He was sitting alone at the table next to me, and we started talking. He moved over to my table, and we ended up eating together," Goldie says bouncing up and down on the bed next to me.

"That's nice. What time is it?"

"Um, eight am."

"And you've already been to breakfast? What is the world coming to?"

"I couldn't sleep. I got up and had to get out of the room. I didn't want to wake you up, so I was extra quiet. Thank goodness I still did my makeup in the bathroom with the door closed so the light wouldn't bother you…"

"Anyway. Tell me about this man you met."

"Are you sitting down? Oh yeah. You're lying down. Well, guess what color his hair is? Guess!"

"Maybe it's…"

"Red! It's red! Like Cam's! I mean he looks like Cam, too. I would have thought he was his brother, but I remembered Katherine saying he was in the big house or something like that. Don't worry, I asked him if he knew a guy named Cam, and he said he didn't, but he's so handsome like Cam. Built like Cam. The body of an athlete. You know how I love that! A doppelganger, isn't that what they call it when someone looks like someone else, but they're not related?"

"Take a breath, Goldie. You are buzzing! What's his name?"

"Kris. Kris with a K. Kris Topher. Isn't that amazing! Put them together, Kris Topher. Get it?"

"He has inventive parents to say the least."

"He's staying here for a break. Kris is from not too far away, Green Bay, Wisconsin, which I guess is five hours away. He tried out for their football team as a kicker. You know, the guy who kicks field goals. He was a free agent I think he said, but he got cut. I guess they already had a kicker they liked or something, and it bummed him out. He's not sure what he wants to do next, but he's letting go of the whole football thing. Their loss is my gain, because he's here, and I got to meet him!"

"You learned a lot in a simple breakfast. He's not married, is he?"

"No, he's not married. He's just an amazingly handsome guy— an amazing athlete— who wanted a break from life. He used to come here as a kid, so he thought this was the place to go. Now, don't go into your suspicious nature about everyone and everything. He's a young, handsome gorgeous man with red hair who is here on vacation, and I like him."

"Okay. I can see you are really taken by him. When do I get to meet him?"

"Tonight, at dinner! He is here alone, so he can come to dinner. I said we would meet him in the lobby at 6:30 pm. So don't be late," she says.

"How long is he here for? Most people only stay for a few days. You don't want to get your hopes up and—"

"He said he can stay as long as he wants. His grandparents passed and left him a boat load of money, so he's not on anyone's timeline. See, he's like us? He's supported by grandparents," she says.

"I mean, shouldn't he be a little more ambitious? Like be thinking about getting a decent job?"

"Stop it, Gilda. I know what you're doing. Putting your stipulations on my future, and I won't have it. He did have something he was doing. He was trying to make it on a pro team, and he didn't. Now he's weighing his options and that's smart. Kris doesn't want to jump into anything. He might go back to college and get a master's degree. He's not sure. And you better not grill him at dinner. Do you promise?"

"Well, I mean, when you are getting to know someone, you ask about their life."

"Yes, but you better do it as you would with any person you are getting to know. Not putting him under the heat lamp, because you're trying to find something wrong with him."

"Alright. Did you tell him you're rich?"

"Oh, so no one can like me for me, huh. Is that it?"

"I didn't say that…"

"Well for your information, I did not tell him I was rich. I told him I'm here doing research for a book I may be writing on vacation islands in the U.S. And that you are here, because you will be illustrating the book. What do you think of that? I didn't tell him I'm rich. So there!"

"Okay. As much as I'm not a fan of lying, at least you've finally heard me about not letting people know you are rich. Then if he likes you, you *can* know it's for you and not for your money," I say, relieved she listened to me for once.

"So, remember tonight, you are the illustrator of my book. I mean, that's entirely possible. You do love to paint," she says.

"I'll remember. Just slow your horses a little bit. You just met him. Get to know him before you're ready to head down the aisle."

"I know. I know. It's just that I've never been a big redhead fan, and then I met Cam, which changed my perspective, and then I met Kris. It's kismet. It's meant to be."

"I'm happy for you. Where are you going now?"

"Are you kidding? I made a hair appointment. A nail appointment. I'm going to look for a new dress. He's not going to forget who he had dinner with tonight. I'll be busy all day, so we can't hang out. What are you doing today?"

"Since I'm now an illustrator of the soon-to-be published book on islands in the U.S,— I better brush up on my artwork. I think I'll do some painting or maybe I'll even stop into The Creative Lilac again," I say, trying to make her feel good.

"Yes! That's the spirit. I can finally stop thinking about Cam and think about Kris. Wait until you see how much they look alike! Would we have redheaded children? Too bad Piper and Cam don't have kids, then I would know what happens when a blonde marries a redhead…"

"Goldie. Again. Slow down!"

She giggles. "Ha! That one was just to get you riled up. It's so easy."

"I don't need to be riled up. I'm still confused about how much I like Remi but feel suspicious of the guy he talked to. And does Katherine have someone watching us? And what are they watching for? We aren't spies. Honestly, I'm still miffed at how Katherine talked about Cam and Piper. They are genuinely nice people. I'd like to spend more time with them."

"Then go see them. Who is stopping you?"

"Not you. You are busy today."

"Oh, did you want to get your hair and nails done? I bet they could work you in…"

"Uh, no. The times I've had an official hair styling I ended up looking like Bride of Frankenstein, which come to think of it, was not too far off from Katherine's very bizarre hairdo," I say finally sitting up and swinging my legs over the side of the bed.

"Well, I'm off. Isn't life grand? You're all bummed out and then a simple breakfast changes your entire world. This truly is 'somewhere in time,' a magical island," she says heading for the door.

She's positively floating. I don't think I've ever been that crazy for a guy. Well, not since Tommy. Ugh. I've worked hard these past few years to completely forget Tommy. Seeing the movie *Somewhere in Time* here at the Grand the other night and then being where they filmed this highly romantic picture has stirred up all my memories of my one true love.

CHAPTER EIGHT

I'm happy for Goldie. I am. She deserves to enjoy that "gee it's great to be alive" feeling as long as she wants. I don't want to be the raincloud on her happy parade.

Tommy. No matter how hard I concentrate on not thinking about you, there you are. Boy, did I fall hard. Everything about you was perfect. The handsome looks, the beautiful eyes, the strong arms.

I remember our first meeting. Like a cliché in a romcom, we both reached for the same book. The library felt like the safest place to spend time together. Heaven knows a public library is the last place Goldie or Granny would be. A place to be free and not worry about prying eyes watching my every move. The library and the coffee shop next door so we didn't have to talk in whispers, those were our special places. I thought I had it covered, always making sure to be in front of the library before the limo came to pick me up. I always said my goodbyes before the ride came and left some time for you to leave and not see a chauffeur opening the door for me. I wanted you to like me, for me, not because I appeared wealthy.

Life, literature, art, we talked about everything. You were one of the few people outside of Goldie who made me laugh.

Really laugh. You told me about your life, growing up very poor and how you wanted to be the one to change that in your family. "Change our futures," that's what you talked about, making something of yourself by studying non-stop.

The more we talked, the more I fell in love with you. That day, when I went to see you, I was going to tell you to run away with me. But that day, you didn't show up at our usual meeting place in the history aisle. I waited and waited and then sat at the coffee shop waiting again. I can't believe in all that time I never got your phone number. I couldn't give you mine because if you called, we would be found out. I didn't know where you lived other than it was a rough area of town. I didn't even know your last name. Honestly, it felt like it added to the romance I thought we were both feeling, at least I *thought* we were. I was so dumb.

So many thoughts went through my mind as I kept going back hoping you would show up. What if you had been in an accident? What if you were in the hospital and needed me? I cried nonstop. Finally, Goldie insisted I tell her what was going on. That's when she decided to make it her mission to find out if a hunch she had was true.

Some strategic eavesdropping got her the answer she suspected. You didn't disappear, Tommy, if that is even your name. You were paid a large amount of money to leave and never contact me again. When Goldie told me she had overheard Granny's phone conversation making sure all the "loose ends" were tied up with the riffraff at the library, she knew she was right.

I know the happiness of thinking you have found someone special. I can't begrudge my sister her giddy moments with Kris. My moments with you, Tommy, were the happiest I had in my life. Even the sting of realizing you loved money more than me can't diminish how much I cherish those beginning times. The precious moments of feeling what it is like to genuinely love someone that way. It is exactly like *Somewhere in Time.* The intense love between the Jane Seymour and Christopher Reeve characters is something everyone wants.

It's taken me a good two years to finally give up on the idea that I would find you, forgive you, and we would be together. This is also the reason I know beyond a doubt that Granny always has eyes watching us and is always making sure we fit in with the plan she has. It's been two more years of intentionally not thinking about you. All in all, the whole thing left me feeling like I lived on Loser Road next to Pathetic Street and my zip code is all zeros. Goldie's reaction to meeting Kris today has brought back all those tender feelings. But I'm happy for her. Now to make sure Granny's spies don't ruin something beautiful in her life the way they ruined it for me. And I'll never be that stupid again.

CHAPTER NINE

"*D*o I look perfect?"

She's looking at herself from every possible angle in the mirror. As if Goldie could ever look anything less than fantastic, even in sweatpants.

"Yes. You look perfect. There isn't one thing you could do differently. He's going to love how you look, what you're wearing...and everything about you," I say hoping I don't have to repeat this five more times.

"Do you like that I chose a lilac-colored dress? Should I have gone with black? It's more slimming...more elegant..."

"More like you're going to a funeral," I say.

"Oh, stop it. You know lots of those movie stars wear black to the Academy Awards," she says never taking her eyes off her reflection in the mirror.

"Besides, you don't need anything 'slimming,' you have the perfect figure. Any color works on you," I say.

"Okay. If you're sure. Hey, you didn't tell me what you ended up doing today?" Goldie asks.

"I stopped in at The Creative Lilac. I could look at those art supplies repeatedly, because I love the variety the store has. I also wanted to know if they had the sign up for an evening class Piper told me about. I'm a little hesitant, because Monsieur Remi had said he wanted to take the class when I first met him. I'm not sure if he's someone I must watch out for. Like is he a Granny spy, or just a guy with a shifty looking business associate? Or am I overthinking everything and being paranoid? Heaven knows, she likes to keep us that way."

"Either way, it can't hurt to take the class. It's not like he can do anything while you're there. You'll be busy painting and maybe you won't even talk to him. Do you think I should add a little more blush?"

"*More* blush? No. Anyway, I did sign up for the class. I got to talk with Piper again. Did I tell you she put a Bible in with my first set of supplies I got?"

"A Bible? Like the ones in church?"

"Yes, a Bible. She has a get-together I guess where people come and study the Bible before the class every week, which she also invited me to. I politely declined of course," I say.

"Of course. Yawn. Can you imagine anything more boring than Shakespeare and the Bible. Thee, thou, this, and that. I mean, I never read it, but I can imagine it's a super snooze."

"The one she gave me is a modern version, with language like we talk. She did say something that stuck with me. It was something along the lines of; it's one thing to reject being a Christian if you've read the Bible, but to reject it when you've never read the Bible—that's a different story," I say.

"I guess that's fair."

"What religion are we? I mean, we are Christian, aren't we?" I ask.

"Well, we're not anything else, so I guess that makes us that. I mean, the few funerals we went to were in a normal church. Mostly we ascribe to the gospel of Granny—the Lord helps those who help themselves! I heard her say that once. Besides, we already have Granny rules driving us crazy; the last thing we need is more dos and don'ts," Goldie says.

"What about heaven? Do you think there is a heaven and a hell?"

"As much as there are fairies and gnomes. It's the kind of thing people believe to make themselves feel better about dying. Probably when we die, we come back as a plant or a flower. I'd pick to return as marigolds. Golden marigolds which partially have my name. Aren't the marigolds here on the island amazing? I imagine I'm a princess and all the little marigolds are my little minions ready to do my bidding. Ahhh, life. What about you? What flower would you come back as?"

"Daisies. Definitely daisies. But I don't think we will come back as flowers. I like to think Mom is up in heaven watching over us. I like that thought," I say quietly.

"That is a nice thought. Besides, we are good people. I'm sure if there is heaven, you just have to have been more nice than not nice, and bingo—you're in. That makes the most sense.

Where is this Bible, she gave you?"

"Where did I put it? Oh, yeah. I have it under this book I'm reading about Hollywood wives."

"Yeah, that sounds much more intriguing."

"Piper said even if I didn't read it now, I would be glad I had it, because I would want to read it at some point or something like that," I say.

"That's a weird thing to say. She probably gets points or gold stars if she gets you to believe in her religion," Goldie says, adding more blush.

"I said *less* blush, Goldie! You had it perfect before. No, she's not like that. I really like her. She is authentic, sweet, and seems like a genuinely good person. Makes me realize how many not-so-good people I've run into..."

"Gilda! The rule of blush is you can *never* have enough blush. I know how to make it just right. Haven't I taught you anything about the world of makeup? So. Are you going to read the book...the Bible?"

"There's a fine line between the right amount of makeup

and looking like a clown," I say handing her a tissue which she knows is for wiping off some blush. "Am I going to read the Bible? I don't know. She said to begin with a book called John. In that book I would learn all about Jesus."

"Oh, remember those crazy Jesus people we saw at the airport in Chicago that time? Jesus People USA or something like that. I'll never understand how people fall into that whole thing. I mean if you want to have a religion, fine. But keep it to yourself. The rest of us just want to have a fun life. They're probably all cults. Okay, I may take off a skoosh of blush. Just a skoosh."

"And when I saw her today, she invited us to go to church with her tomorrow morning at the Little Stone Church. You know the one we pass when we head into town?" I ask.

"Oh, that's a real church? Not a museum?"

"It's a church, and they have a service at 10 am."

"Well, I hope you made up an excuse."

"I left it kind of open ended, saying I would check with you."

"Negatory. You can go if you want but not my cup of tea. Speaking of tea, I couldn't get that tea stain out of my shirt, so I threw it away," Goldie says.

"Goldie. I know we have money, but wow. You only wore it once. I could have tried to get the stain out. Is it already gone in the trash?"

"Yup. The maid took the trash out earlier. Bye-bye blouse."

"Listen, as you get to know Kris, be careful about sounding too rich, even if you don't say it. You want him to like you for you," I say.

"I know. We've been over this. I'm an author, remember? That's how we get our money. Be nice to your sister. I'm fairly sure that's in the Bible. Thou shalt not bug your sister causing her to want to bean you with a pillow!"

"Oh, okay," I say laughing. "You're lucky you're all ready to go or there would be a pillow coming your way."

"Come on. I don't want to keep my Prince Charming waiting. I can't wait for you to meet him. Goldie Topher! Doesn't that have a nice ring to it?" Goldie says heading for the door. "You could have used a little more blush."

"Why don't you start a blush company? And stop jumping ahead with this guy. You need to get to know him before you take his last name," I say, following her out the door to the elevator.

"I know. I only said that so I could see the steam come out of your ears."

"There's enough in life to raise my blood pressure. You don't need to add to it."

Please let me like this Kris Topher. If he seems like a scammer, I will have to get rid of him. Ugh. There may be more of Granny in me than I realize.

CHAPTER TEN

"Do you believe all these choices?" Kris asks.

We've made it through polite introductions and Goldie is right. Kris does have an uncanny resemblance to Cam with the red hair, and yes, he's very handsome. His crisp navy suit and white shirt are accented by a beautiful sea blue tie that matches his eyes. We are seated in the Salle à Manger, the big title on the doorway we see as we walk into the huge dining room. Goldie found out the words mean a room in a home or hotel where people eat meals. In other words: dining room. We're all paying attention to the menu as the waiter heads toward our table. Well, Kris and I are looking at the menu. Goldie only has eyes for Kris.

"Okay, what are you both doing in the appetizer category? Sparking passionfruit and peach juice, roasted heirloom carrots, pork belly and rabbit terrine...oh wow, that comes with sourdough and apricot mustard, and let's see... butternut squash ravioli or seared jumbo day boat scallop," Kris says reading off the menu.

"And that's just the appetizer! There's an interesting soup choice, salad choices...I'm leaning toward the warm beet salad...and then the main courses. Charred savoy cabbage, maple-glazed cedar plank salmon, pretzel-crusted chicken breast, pan-roasted duck breast, and surf and turf. I've never heard of using pretzels as breading for chicken," I say.

"Isn't this room something else? Gorgeous, really. I love the ambiance, the piano quartet playing, the china and linens with the geraniums on them. Speaking of gorgeous. You both look lovely tonight," Kris says.

"Thank you," Goldie says leaning in toward him even further.

He sure pays attention to details. Could be a good trait in a person, I suppose.

I love the cordial waiters we've had since being on the island. A lovely gentleman takes our order, and I get to hear my new favorite phrase, "milady" as he takes my order.

"Would you like a roll?" I ask passing the basket of golden goodness filled with several types of fresh-baked biscuits and breads. "Goldie tells me you used to come here as a kid."

"Oh, yes, thanks. I'd love a roll. Yes, to answer your question, a trip or two. But I didn't get to see all the sights I wanted. So, this trip, I want to see everything I can. I enjoy history and there's a rich history here. I was reading about the Little Stone Church just down the avenue here. Did you notice the stone? It was built in 1904, and I really want to see the stain glass windows inside. They depict some of the history of Mackinac Island," he says.

"It's so funny you say that because some new friends we met here on the island invited us to go to church there tomorrow. They own The Creative Lilac, an art store downtown. But Goldie doesn't—" before I can finish the sentence Goldie gives me a kick under the table and takes over my sentence.

"Goldie told you she would love to go to the church with them, because she's been dying to see the inside as well! Don't you remember Gilda when I asked you if you noticed the beautiful stones on that church? Honestly, Kris, sometimes she forgets so fast!"

Okay, sister. Throw me under the bus the minute a guy enters the picture.

"Uh, yes. I did forget your keen interest in the Little Stone Church. It must have slipped my mind. So, then, you would like to go? And Kris, I'm sure they wouldn't mind if you came along, too," I say.

"Why not? Sounds perfect. Why don't we all have brunch after church with your friends, and then, if you ladies agree, I would like to rent a horse and carriage with a guide to take us to see some more sights on the island. Would you like to do that?" Kris asks.

"Yes. That sounds perfect!" Goldie says batting her eyes like she's in a 1940s romance flick.

"I think it would be great to meet some local island people and get their take on what to see before we head out on adventure," Kris says.

"That's nice of you, Kris. I don't know if Piper and Cam, those are the names of the people we were talking about, are free for brunch, but we can certainly invite them," I say.

"Here's your first course!" Our wonderful waiter serves us our choices.

As we settle into the delicious meal, I see how happy Kris makes Goldie. He seems like a genuinely nice young man. Very polished. Quite unlike the guys Goldie usually gravitates toward. Maybe she will get the beginning of a *Somewhere in Time* true romance for herself. At least one of us should experience a happily ever after.

CHAPTER ELEVEN

"We're so happy you could join us for church this morning!" Piper says giving me a hug.

Gathered outside of the Little Stone Church on this beautiful Sunday morning, I'm not sure if I want to be here. I do want to get to know Cam and Piper more, and this seems important to them, but I don't want to sit through a boring church service. Once Goldie was on board, only for the reasons of pleasing Kris, it seemed a good idea. Now that we're all here, I should make the best of it. Church will be for a short time and then we can get onto brunch and have some fun. And I do want to see the inside of this historic place.

"Thank you for inviting us. Cam and Piper, you remember my sister Goldie, and this is her friend Kris Topher," I say as Cam and Kris shake hands.

"My goodness. Kris! You look like—" Piper starts to say.

"Me!" Cam interjects.

"I see it, too," Kris says.

"The red hair does add to it, but I think we are the same size, color of eyes. I've never met someone who could be my double," Cam says with a big laugh.

"What's that called when that happens?" Piper asks.

"Doppelganger," Goldie says. "I thought the same thing. Kris looks like Cam or Cam looks like Kris."

"I'm probably a little older," Cam says.

"I'm twenty-two," Kris says.

"Yes, I have a few years on you, but we are very similar." Cam says. "And Gilda told us you tried out for the Packers? That's my team! We will have to talk about that!"

"Oh, you're a fan? Interesting. Not to rush things, but I'm really looking forward to seeing those stained-glass windows," Kris says looking toward the church entrance.

"Yes, of course. Let's get inside and get seated. The regular pastor is gone this weekend. We are friends with the visiting pastor who is taking his place. He always has such insightful things to share," Piper says heading toward the opening doors.

Taking our seats, I do like the peaceful vibe I'm feeling. This place is much smaller and more intimate than the few big churches I've been in. This is the most I've thought about church and religion in my whole life. I hope they tell you when to do whatever it is you're supposed to do.

"Welcome everyone. It's always a pleasure to be here on Mackinac Island. I'm Pastor Tim. It's good to see my friends Cam and Piper here this morning. I'm excited to share from God's Word today, but first, let's turn to page twenty-nine in your hymnal and sing *Amazing Grace* together."

Everyone stands up, and we all sing the song on the page. So far, so good. No faux pas from the Lock sisters to this point. Wow, these stained-glass windows are amazing, showing scenes from long ago on the island the colors are…wait! There's Remi two rows behind us to the left. He doesn't strike me as someone who goes to church, but then, I have nothing to base that on. Maybe Piper and Cam invited him, too? Okay. They said to "be seated." The pastor says to turn in our Bibles to Luke. Go to the tenth chapter, and he'll read verses forty-one through forty-two.

Oh boy. I think I can count this as reading the Bible if Piper asks me if I read it. Score! Get your mind off Remi, Gilda, and listen to what this guy has to say. Maybe it can add into my being a "good person" and score me points for heaven. He has a nice speaking voice.

"Here's today's scripture. '*Martha, Martha,*' *the Lord answered, 'you are worried and upset about many things, but few things are needed—or indeed only one. Mary has chosen what is better and it will not be taken away from her,*" the pastor says looking up.

"If you aren't familiar with this story in the Bible, let me give you a little background. This story takes place at the home of Lazarus and his sisters, Martha and Mary. These siblings were good friends of Jesus. Some speculate that with Martha being the older sister, she was the head of the household and was most likely used to being in charge. They were probably a wealthy family with a place large enough to accommodate Jesus and his disciples.

"Jesus was teaching and speaking to the gathered group at their home, which included His disciples. Meanwhile, Martha was busy making sure her guests were comfortable and well fed. Instead of helping, Martha's sister Mary, was sitting at Jesus's feet, listening to what He was saying.

"Picture it. Martha is probably hot and tired from unexpected guests arriving. They couldn't phone ahead to say they were coming," the pastor says.

That brought a chuckle from the people.

"As probably you or I would have done, Martha asks Jesus why He doesn't care that her sister is sitting there while she is left to do all the work herself. You have to realize in those days it was unheard of for a woman to sit at a rabbi's feet and listen to him teach. Most girls of the day were illiterate and worked in the home," the pastor explains.

"Remember, too, that these siblings were friends with Jesus. They didn't know at this point all that was going to follow, that He would die and rise again. So, Martha very comfortably says to her friend, what gives? Look at what's happening. Have a talk with my sister, please!"

This guy is really good.

"This is when we get to the Bible verses we read today. Jesus tells her, as a friend talking to a friend, patiently and calmly, she is focusing on the wrong things. Mary sees there is only one thing to focus on, and I won't take it away from her. What can we get out of this as people living in 1984 in these modern times? Are there truths from this story that apply to us today? The answer is yes, as in most things we read in the Bible."

Stuff in the Bible for today, too? Hmmmm.

"First, Jesus is making the point that being His disciple and learning from His teachings is the most important thing we can do. Everything else is secondary. Next, he addresses her worry and anxiety. Had she gone to Jesus, He would have advised her and helped her work through what was troubling her without her experiencing worry and being upset with her sister. He would have pointed out that Mary was not being lazy, she simply had her priorities straight for that moment," the pastor says.

That's an interesting way to look at it. This guy isn't anything like the monotone stuff I've heard at funerals.

"There's our lesson. Instead of worrying about everything, let's go to Jesus and have Him work it out with us and for us. That's a gift He has given us as our loving Savior. We need time with Him, every day. To sit at His feet so we can live this life here on earth with joy and abundance no matter the circumstances of life. That's what we can know as children of a loving God, someone who gives us a forever family. This story reminds me of a verse in Matthew, and I'll close with this thought: 'But seek first the kingdom of God and his righteousness, and all these things will be added to you,' Matthew 6:33."

Wow. These people really get a lot out of reading the Bible. I don't know if I would have taken that much out of it on my own.

"You've been a wonderfully, attentive congregation this morning. Let's pray and close with a hymn," the pastor says.

At the last amen, we all stand. Piper is right. I guess I don't know much about what's really in a Bible. I mean, I don't want to become a religious nut or anything, but that pastor gave me so much to think about.

"Bonjour, Gilda. It's so nice to see you here today. I very much enjoyed ze sermon. Did you?" asks Remi.

I didn't see him come toward me. or I would have been faster to elude him.

"Yes, it was interesting. Have a good day," I say, hurrying away to meet the others who have already gone through the door. Catching up to Piper, she has an inquisitive look on her face.

"Was that Monsieur Remi at church? I should go back and say hello," she says turning back toward the door.

"You know what! I bet the restaurants get busy around here after church. We better all head on out so we get a table. Come on everyone! Let's head into town for brunch and get a seat before they all fill up." I say, herding them together and pushing us on the sidewalk toward town.

Thankfully, they all follow like lost sheep. Glancing back, I see Remi speaking with the pastor just outside the door. Good. Stay preoccupied. There's no way I trust you, even if you did go to church.

CHAPTER TWELVE

"You're the closest Cam has ever come to meeting a Packers player. I have to keep him in check or all he'll talk about is football," Piper says. "But truth be told, I'm a big Packers fan, too."

"Aren't you fans of the Michigan team?" Kris asks.

"Can't even bring yourself to say the word Lions, huh? Technically, being in the Upper Peninsula, you'll find fans of both teams. Lower Michigan is much more Lions' fans, but here, it's divided. Football wasn't even on my radar until I married Cam. I saw how much he loved it. So, I started watching, and he was nice enough to explain the game to a newbie like me. Eventually, I came to understand what is happening, and I've come to love those crazy games, too. Many times, I'm biting my nails with close scores, but overall, it's a fun thing we do together," Piper says.

"I don't know much about football, but now I'm definitely interested in learning more about the game," Goldie says batting her eyelashes at Kris.

Please, Goldie. You couldn't care less about football. Geesh. She is head over heels for this guy.

"Oh, yeah. I've consistently kicked field goals from the fifty-yard line," Kris says.

"The fifty yard line? Wow! And that's not really fifty yards, because there's ten yards to the end zone and the hold is seven yards behind the center, so really, more like sixty-seven yards! Incredible! You have to keep trying to get on a team if you can do those kinds of kicks," Cam says.

"Oh, well, maybe I'm bragging too much. I tend to choke under pressure," Kris says.

His face is a bit red. Is he embarrassed, because he's so good but still didn't make the team?

"My favorite is a pick-six. It makes the game so exciting!" Piper says.

"Yeah, they should always pick the six best guys to play on the team," Kris says.

Piper and Cam burst out laughing, but I don't get the joke.

"Good one Kris!" Cam says.

"You're the pro Kris; you explain it to them," Piper says still giggling.

"I've got to use the restroom; I'll let you guys explain," Kris says, getting up and heading toward the back of the restaurant.

For some reason, he's not laughing. I hope they didn't hurt his feelings. He seems very raw about not making the team.

"I didn't know what a pick-six was before I started watching the games either," Piper says. "It's an interception. In other words, the quarterback throws it to someone on his team, and someone from the other team catches it instead and then runs it back to his own goal for a touchdown. It's always super exciting and gets the crowd going crazy."

"Maybe we should change the subject. Too much football talk seems to be making Kris a little uncomfortable," I say glancing toward the bathroom.

"I'm so sorry. That's very insensitive of us. Not making the team must have been devastating, and you did say he came here to get away from it. Oh boy, Cam. We were thinking about ourselves, not him. I'm going to apologize when he returns," Piper says.

"Absolutely. I wasn't thinking about his feelings," Cam says.

"I think it's better to just be talking about something else and let it drop," I say.

"Again, so sorry. We didn't mean to offend anyone," Piper says.

"You had no idea. Don't feel bad, really. Now I feel dumb I said anything," I say.

Learn when to be quiet Gilda! Am I reading this all wrong? Kris seemed agitated, but I could be imagining it.

"I'm so bored with that whole conversation anyway. I'm happy to change the topic," Goldie says. "Oh, look, here comes Mr. Handsome now.

"What did I miss?" Kris asks.

"Not a thing. Did you know that Kris rented a horse and carriage for us to take a tour of the island this afternoon? What do you think is a 'must see' from your viewpoint?" Goldie asks, turning to Cam and Piper.

"Oh, there are so many things not to miss. I would say make sure to stop at the natural rock formations including Arch Rock, Sugar Loaf, and the crack in the island. And don't miss the beauty of the interior woods and paths, something that gets lost in the glamour of the individual sites. I'm so glad you are doing that. You're going to love it," Piper says.

"I picked up a nice map at the concierge area of the Grand Hotel, so they shouldn't be too hard to find," Kris says.

"Yes, it's only eight miles around the island, so even if you get lost in the interior, you'll enjoy it," Cam says.

"What did you think about the service this morning?" Piper asks.

"Oh, I've never been to anything like it," I say.

"Me either," Goldie says. "We've only been in really big

churches for a few funerals. The windows inside there were pretty."

"I really enjoyed seeing the architecture and the stained-glass windows. That's what I was so looking forward to and it didn't disappoint," Kris says.

"I thought it was cool that the pastor talked about sisters in the Bible, and here you are, sisters," Piper says.

It seems like she wants to talk about the sermon. Good luck with this crew.

"I for one want to hear about how you and Cam met, and how you ended up getting married and living on the island," Goldie says.

Subtle Goldie. I know your agenda. Hook the man.

"Well, that's a long story of how I came here from San Francisco and ended up staying, mostly because of meeting Cam. We had a whirlwind romance and in hindsight, got married very quickly," Piper says.

"And look how happy you are even after a 'whirlwind romance' as you call it. Just shows that when you know, you know. Seems like magical relationships often start on this enchanting island," Goldie says so obviously smiling at Kris.

"They do," Cam says with a chuckle. "But Piper and I have talked a lot about how much we didn't know about each other before we got married. It led to some rough moments in our first year, for sure. Honestly, if it hadn't been for our dedication to living our lives for Jesus, and putting Him first, we might not both be sitting with you here today."

Thank goodness. That should slow Goldie down, because I'm sure that's not what she wanted to hear. I guess, I didn't expect them to be so honest about the trials of marriage. They seem like the fairy tale of happily ever after who skipped the reality of two people trying to get along past the honeymoon stage.

Oh, good. Here's our food. We need to get out of the awkward mode we've fallen into. This has been quite a morning.

I want to tell Piper that talk at church wasn't lost on me. I have so many questions. So many questions. But I'll save them for another time. As Piper catches my gaze, I give her a wink. I hope she knows I want to know more about what gets her through life. There has to be more than living under Granny's thumb.

CHAPTER THIRTEEN

Kris seems perkier as our tour guide. I'm glad he's not afraid of driving the carriage. That's one "rich girl" skill neither Goldie nor I ever really took to—equestrians. The brochures Goldie brought help us understand what we are seeing. It's fun taking turns reading facts as we go from one site to the next.

"Did you know, Michilimackinac, gosh I hope I said that right, means Place of the Great Turtle. The native Americans called it that because of how the island rose out of the water like a turtle. There are many limestone bluffs that make up the island," Goldie says reading from a brochure.

"I do see little turtle statues and references to turtles around the island. Now I get it," I say.

"Listen to this. While Yellowstone was the first national park, the second one was Mackinac Island. How about that?" Goldie says.

"So, it's a national park?" I ask.

"No, it goes on to say that when Fort Mackinac was decommissioned in 1895, the land was handed over to the state of Michigan. It lost its national park status but gained a new one; Michigan's first state park. Eighty-two percent of the land on the island is a state park. But the park still looks very similar to how it looked in 1895," Goldie says looking up to see Kris's reaction.

"That is interesting. You should be a tour guide, Goldie," Kris says rewarding her with a big smile.

If it's possible for a person to shoot sunbeams out of their head, it's happening with Goldie. She sure wants this man's attention. I have no idea how I'm going to pull her back from this. Hopefully, Kris will only stay a short time, and the separation will naturally dissolve. The more I hear him talk, the more he doesn't strike me as a guy looking for a commitment. And she is on the hunt, big time. Maybe she thinks he's rich enough to give her the life she wants without Granny, but I doubt it. His clothes are fine, but they aren't the designer brands that boys raised in money wear. He's handsome but not polished. Even though he mentioned his grandparents leaving him money, I'm sure it's not the money we are used to. I'm happy to be cordial but I see the writing on the wall. Kris is a momentary pleasure, not a real, lifelong consideration.

"Penny for your thoughts?" Kris says looking at me.

"Oh, sorry. I'm lost in the beauty of everything we're seeing, and the gentle clip clop of these magnificent horses. You are so good at driving a carriage," I say.

"Thank you. I'm really enjoying the variety of horses here on the island. It's been one of the favorite parts of my stay," he says.

"Do you expect to be here the entire rest of the season? I mean, the leaves get prettier every day," I say, hoping I'm not being too obvious. "Weren't they pretty this morning in front of the Little Stone Church?"

"I noticed that, too. Yes, amazing. To answer your question, I'm not sure. I'm taking it day by day."

Darn. I was hoping he had plans to leave soon.

"Good thing you have that inheritance, because it sure is not the most inexpensive place to stay for a get away," I say.

What is his gig anyway?

"That's true! I'm amazed you ladies can stay here with no end date in sight while you work on your book! That must be one big advance you received from the publisher to be able to afford it," he says with a look back at me I don't like.

Oh. So, you don't like my questions, and you are trying to throw them back in my face. Well, there's a devious little side to you I haven't seen before, but then, what do we really know about you, Kris Topher?

"Gilda! Quit talking about leaving when we are all having so much fun on this ride," Goldie says, giving me a sister look I know which means—shut up!

"Yeah, Gilda. Lighten up. Say, shouldn't you be sketching some of these places for your book?" Kris says.

I'm really starting to not like him!

"Oh, I do my sketching later in my room. I'm taking it all in. This ride will help greatly with my ideas for the book," I say looking over at Goldie.

Thanks, Goldie. This lie is coming back to bite us. Next, he's going to want to know why you aren't spending any time writing.

As beautiful as the ride has been, I'm ready to have some separation from this Bogie and Bacall duo. When we arrive at the carriage rental, I'm happy to walk back to the Grand. I don't mind moving a little faster and letting them lag behind. A nice little nap sounds good if I can fit one in before dinner. Climbing the steps up to the porch, I see him out of the corner of my eye. If I go quickly, he may not see me.

"Gilda! Gilda!" Remi says standing up and calling out to me from the table he's filled with his paper and paint supplies. "Come and see what I'm painting."

Drat. Goodbye nap. Hello Remi. This is one conversation I didn't want to have.

CHAPTER FOURTEEN

"I'm so happy you happened by! I was hoping to see you and see if you have begun painting yet. This is my first time painting on ze porch here at ze Grand and I'm enjoying it very much. This is one of ze most beautiful places to paint natural beauty," Remi says, gesturing to all the paints and paper on his table.

Is this the place to confront him or do I look at his paintings and move on? Wouldn't that be much easier?

"You are doing an amazing job. I see you've been working on Round Island Lighthouse. Really nice!" I say.

"Yes, and I can't wait for ze class with Piper to learn even more about making ze water move. Have you begun to do some painting?"

"No, not yet. I've been visiting, shopping, and spending time with my sister," I say.

Okay. Skip it. Say goodbye, get upstairs, and see if you can get a nap.

"Gilda. I don't know what I did to offend you so greatly," Remi says.

Or not. I guess this is happening.

"You didn't do anything specifically, but I've had some

strange things happen in my life, and I have to be cautious. The gentlemen you spoke to and then left so quickly at Piper's store that day, well, he looked a little ominous. That scared me. I seem to see you wherever I am. You were even at church this morning," I say.

"So, you think I'm following you, no?"

"Maybe. I mean, were you going to church this morning or did you find out I was going?"

"I had no way to know if you were going to ze church. I try to go to church every Sunday, and this church was so close to ze hotel. It made ze most sense," he says with a look of concern in his eyes.

"Oh, I see."

"As far as the man who spoke to me at ze store, he is my lawyer who is doing some investigative work for me and my business while I am here. Yes, he looks a little, as you say, ominous, but he's a perfectly nice gentleman. He's very serious when he is working."

"And it's certainly not my business to know your business. Maybe I've been overreacting. At the elevator that day, you were also…"

"Oui, oui. I can see how you would see it that way. My apologies. I was hoping we could be friends, especially as we love ze painting. But if you are more comfortable, I can leave you alone. I didn't want to cause you any harm or despair. This was not my intention," Remi says. "In fact, I can withdraw my name from Piper's classes if that would make you more comfortable."

"Like I said, I am most likely jumping to conclusions. You have the right to go anywhere on the island and to any class you want to. Forgive me. I have a lot on my mind. There's no problem with us being in the same art class. That would be silly."

"I will try to be more, well, how can I say this in English, less creepy? Is that what I mean?"

He has such kind eyes. I think I have been way off. And rude. I've been rude to a perfectly nice person.

"I'm sorry Remi. Really, I am. I look forward to taking the class with you. You are doing some lovely work here. I can only hope to do something half as good as you have going with your Round Island Lighthouse," I say.

"No comparison. We each bring our own gift to God's good earth."

What a lovely thing to say.

"Did you enjoy ze sermon this morning?" Remi asks.

"I haven't had a moment to give it much thought, but yes, it was very insightful. You said you go to church every Sunday?"

"Yes. For several years now. I wasn't always this way, but when I started to understand that Jesus died for each of us, I began to explore ze Bible for myself."

"Really? Piper put a Bible in my art order. She encouraged me to read it. Truthfully, I had no interest at all, but after today, I am more intrigued."

"She put one in my order, too, but I already own several. I'm going to return it, so she can give it to someone else who doesn't have one."

"That's nice of you. Listen I have to get going, because soon they are going to shoo us off to get ready for dinner. And you need a minute to put away all your supplies and get ready yourself," I say glancing at my watch.

"Oui. This is true. Good thing you are paying ze attention. Remember, if you see me at dinner, I am not chasing you. And tonight, I dine with my lawyer, so don't be afraid of him. He is an honorable man. Tonight, I hope to find out some news that may change my life; in fact, it is ze reason I am really here. But that story is for another time, my friend. Enjoy your evening, and if I don't see you before, I'll see you at ze class. Au revoir."

"Au revoir, Remi. I'm glad you stopped me, and we could clear the air. This is much better," I say.

So many conversations today. I think I'll stop down in the

coffee shop and grab a nice strong espresso to bring up to the room while I get ready for dinner. I need the caffeine, because this nap is not happening. Walking down the stairs to the lower level to the little coffee area, once again I'm struck by how gorgeous everything is. We are so lucky to get to stay here so long. I've overhead people saying they could only stay a night or two, and we are here for most of the fall it looks like. I should spend more time enjoying life than judging other people.

Let's see. They have lots of choices. Come on Gilda, make a choice already. I'll take a plain cup of coffee I think out of the pots already made. That will be fast. Okay, perfect liquid, do your thing. I'll catch the elevator, go upstairs, and wait... is that Kris talking to Katherine Sims-Dubois down the hall? Hmmm, if I duck behind this column, they can't see me. I'm not close enough to hear them, but what gives? Hey, I don't think they look like people who just met. That's too animated of a conversation for casual introductions. How does Kris know Katherine? I knew something was off with him. When will I ever learn to trust my gut? I'm usually right.

CHAPTER FIFTEEN

"Finally! I've been waiting for you to get up here ever since Kris walked me to our room. He insisted on walking me to my door; that's how much of a gentleman he is. He said to wait for you and then come down so we can all have a wonderful dinner together. It's almost time, and he will be waiting for us. And did I mention that I'm mad at you, because I didn't like the tone you were using while talking with my boyfriend? He pays for a carriage for us and a lovely afternoon, and you give him attitude. Not cool, sister. Not cool!" Goldie says getting a little louder with each word.

Oh, Lord, if you exist, give me strength.

"A. He's not your boyfriend. 2. I just saw Mr. Wonderful downstairs having what I would call an intimate conversation with one Katherine Sims-Dubois. What do you have to say about that?" I ask.

"So what? He's free to talk to anyone. She told us she makes it a point to know what's happening on the island. He looks so much like Cam she might have thought it was him, approached him, and then realized it wasn't. Like us, she wanted to know more about him. Someone could say we were having an intimate tea with Katherine Sims-Dubois, and you and I both know that wouldn't be the truth!"

Ugh. She has a point there.

"You are just like the bad sister in the story," Goldie says wagging her finger at me.

"What story? Oh, the sermon at the church? Which one was the bad one?"

"The one who had to stay busy, of course. The man said Jesus was happier or something like that with the sister who sat at his feet and listened to what he had to say. The other sister had to stay busy, so much like a busy-body sister I know," she says.

I'm shocked she heard a word of the sermon.

"I'm not sure that's the whole lesson he was trying to teach," I say.

"Oh, because only you can know things, because you're the smart one. I'm the pretty one and you're the smart one. That means I can't hear anything and get something out of it," she says stomping her feet.

"I have never, ever said that to you. And I never would. Yes, you are very pretty, and you are also very smart. I know that. On the other hand, you are the one who finds something at fault with my looks. So let me throw that right back in your face. Just because you're the pretty one, and I'm the smart one, I can't see what's really going on most of the time?"

I'm not sure that's exactly the way to say what I'm thinking, but she should get the meaning.

"Only because then you would have it all! You would be perfect in your looks. A nose job would be just right to finish off what you have started there. You're already smart, so finish the job!" Goldie says.

I have never punched my sister, but this may be the first time.

"You know what you are? You're a narcissist," I say, while pointing at her face.

"Oh, don't forget. I'm the dumb one. What's a narc...sis...whatever?"

"A narcissist is someone who has an exaggerated sense of self-importance. The world revolves around you. Everything must be 'just-right' according to Goldie's standards or watch out," I say.

"Well then, everyone is 'one of those', because everyone thinks in terms of themselves. It's natural. That's how we survive," she says.

"You missed the most important word. An *exaggerated* sense of self-importance. Who does that remind you of? Someone near and dear to you?"

"Don't you even for one second say that to me. That is the meanest thing you have ever said. If anyone is like Granny, it's you. So suspicious of everyone you meet. There are no good people in the world. According to you, everyone has an angle. You can't live in the moment and enjoy life. *We have to get away from Granny...we have to get out on our own...we have to be poor.* You know what? You should do it. You should go out on your own and for the first time, I don't care if we stick together. Right now, I don't care if I ever see you again! I'm going down to dinner to meet Kris, and please don't join us. Eat alone. See how you like it," Goldie says going to the door and slamming it shut on her way out.

Then the tears start. As much as I hate her right now, I don't know what to think. I'm the one who was so suspicious of Remi when he didn't do anything to deserve it. Now I'm suspicious of Kris. Is what she's saying the truth? Am I the one who is most like Granny?

I feel so alone.

Ring, ring.

Ugh, that phone made me jump. Maybe it's Goldie calling from the parlor to apologize and this can be over.

"Hello?"

"Hi, Gilda? It's Piper. I'm just doing a final count on my

class for this week, so I have the right amount of supplies ready. It will be just you, correct? Goldie won't be joining us?"

"Hi Piper. Yes, you're correct. Just me."

"Is everything okay? Are you getting a cold?"

"No. Allergies I guess."

"Gilda, are you sure? You sound…sad."

I can't stop the tears.

"Piper, I just had a huge fight with Goldie, I mean really bad. So, truthfully, I'm crying. She's gone to dinner, and I'm trying to get myself together."

"Oh, I'm so sorry. I don't have any siblings, so I'm not going to pretend I know exactly what you're going through. Do you want to come over to the cottage and talk? Cam has gone to a meeting, and I can rustle up some cheese, crackers, and fruit to munch on. Our place is right at the end of the porch, before all the houses on the bluff. If you need a friend, I'm here for you," Piper says softly.

"You know what? That sounds like something I need more than a big dinner by myself tonight. I need to wash my face and then I'll head over. Does that work for you?"

"Works perfectly. I'll see you soon."

Hanging up I feel a little better. I desperately need a friend right now. Especially since the best friend I had my whole life wants nothing to do with me.

CHAPTER SIXTEEN

If I put my head down and quickly take the steps all the way to the lower level, I should get to the doors on the road that runs in front of the porch. That way, I should be able to avoid "everyone dressed in their finery" as they describe it in the Grand's rules for dress after six pm. I'm staying in my jeans. And most importantly, I can elude Goldie.

There it is, right where she said it was. A sweet little bungalow. I'm nervous. Maybe this isn't a good idea. I don't need to drag someone into our lives when they know so little of our story. It won't make sense without the background of knowing we are raised by a lady who, according to my sister, is part of the mafia. Okay, I'll knock.

As Piper opens the door, I feel better. This sweet, small home is comforting. It's got a bohemian vibe. Her paintings and touches are throughout this cozy room. I love this corner fireplace with a crackling fire.

"Come in and have a seat," Piper says gesturing to her couch set in front of a coffee table with a nice little spread of goodies.

"Is iced tea okay for you, or would you prefer something

else?" she asks as we sit down and fill our cute little plates which are the shape of tulips.

"Iced tea is perfect, and I've never seen plates in the shape of tulips before!" I say.

"I know. I love them. They were a gift from Freddy. He found them in a thrift store and knew they would be perfect for me."

"Listen, I'm sorry to sound so dramatic on the phone," I say.

"You're hurting, Gilda, and you need to talk. Is it because you and Goldie spend so much time together? Just a case of getting on each other's nerves? I know I can't be with Cam all day, every day. I need my space, and he does, too."

"That's part of it. We've been raised in a strange way by our granny who pulls all our purse strings, literally. We live on the allowance she gives us. Going out on our own has always been a bit of a fight, although Goldie is right. Anytime we've tried it, we've failed. If we didn't fail, Granny made sure we did. So, we are a bit lost. The bottom line is we're here not knowing why or for how long. Granny told us to come and here we are. Sounds pathetic to hear my own words out loud. I can't imagine what you think," I say.

"It's not my place to be a judge of anything in anyone else's life. Believe me. My life looks simple now, but that was not always the case. I could tell you some amazing details of my past that would make your jaw drop. The one thing I can offer you, or anyone is to know that God loves you and has a plan for your life. That's where my comfort and peace come from. Bad and hard things still come, but now I have a different viewpoint about them," Piper says.

"I'm remembering you saying at some point I would be happy to have a Bible, and I'm thinking, this may be that time," I say.

Grabbing her Bible on the table, she moves a little closer to me on the couch.

"Let me show you something. Let's go to the book of John I

told you about. It's the story of Jesus, from the time He came here as a baby in a manger, until the time He dies and rises again, and how that affects us all these years later. Let's look up the third chapter and the sixteenth verse. It says:

For God so loved the world that He gave his one and only Son, that whoever believes in Him shall not perish but have eternal life.

"That verse was written for me and for you. To make that even more clear, let's read it again, but this time, let's paraphrase it a little and put our names in there.

For God so loved the world that He gave his one and only Son, that if Gilda and Piper believe in Him, they won't perish but have eternal life.

"Have you ever heard that?" Piper asks.

"Honestly, other than what the pastor read on Sunday and what you read right now, that's the most I've ever heard out of the Bible. Well, except for whatever they say at funerals. I've always heard things as distant. I guess is the word I would use. But the way you read it, that's very personal. Is that your point?"

"Exactly. We were separated from God by sin. He gave us free choice, and people naturally choose sin over living a godly life. He didn't want people in His forever family who were forced to love Him. He wants people who choose to love Him because of who He is. He made it all possible when He sent His only son, Jesus, to die for our sins. He rose again on that third day after His death, because He overcame death. One death for all to have the opportunity to spend forever with Him in heaven, and to live a life here of purpose and meaning with the guidance of His Holy Spirit. He asks us to come to Him with faith, like a little child," Piper says.

"I get that. Listening to what you are saying I have a million questions, but looking at it as a child would look at something is so different. Children take things at face value, something I don't seem to have the ability to do anymore. So, this verse in the Bible is for us, today too."

"Yes. Everyone in their life at some point comes to this moment. Some people hear it as children, some not until they are older. The Bible tells us, everyone does get the choice. When they hear the truth of what Jesus did for them, the question is, what are you going to do with this truth? Do you want to put your name in there, believe and follow Him or do you reject it?"

"That's kind of scary. So, if I don't, I perish and I end up in hell?" I ask.

Surely that's not what she means.

"Jesus says in the Bible that He is the Way, the Truth, and the Life and no one comes to the Father but through Him. This was the plan God put in place to save us."

"So that's what religion is? Making the choice?"

"No. Religion can get bogged down by adding all kinds of extra rules. Now are there many truths and tools we can learn and live by in the Bible that show us how to live like Jesus? There sure are. He gave us everything we need; He's such a loving Savior. But we're talking about something much greater than religion as most people think about it. We're talking about a real, thriving relationship with God the Father, God the Son, and God the Holy Spirit. The Bible also says to those who don't believe it, it sounds foolish and crazy. But to those who do believe it, it's a powerful demonstration of God's love and sacrifice. It's one of the great mysteries of starting to see the world is much more…it's spiritual, not just physical. So, without belief, it will sound odd to you," she says.

"It can't be that simple. I believe and then poof…Heaven," I say.

"There is lots of spiritual growth, lessons and learning after you ask Jesus into your heart, but that first step is amazingly simple. Either He is who He said He is and it's real, or He's the world's biggest liar deceiving people for nearly 2000 years…or however long it's been since he arrived in a manger. I'm terrible at math," Piper says with her sweet smile.

"You know, if anyone else was saying this to me, I'd be running for the door, like someone was trying to get me in a cult. But I don't feel that way with you," I say.

"It's no coincidence I called you tonight, although I didn't know that when I called. I really did want to know about the class. But the Holy Spirit has a way of guiding us. I kept getting this little nudge to call you. What I usually do is ignore it once, but when I get that soft little nudge in my spirit again, I try to act on it. That's how He communicates with us. It can be a verse in the Bible that leaps off the page, and we know He's teaching us something. It can be something a friend says, even if they aren't a believer. It can be when we gather to worship Him in church. It can be a flower that speaks of His beauty in creation. God is not limited in any way from talking with us. God is a God of order, and as I said, beauty. There are no coincidences. There is no such thing as luck. He has a specific plan for each person's life. He knows every person because He created you and me, and His plan is perfect. Now, we are not in a perfect world, so there's also a verse that tells us, we will have trials. We also have someone who hates us, the devil, who wants to destroy anyone who gives their life to Jesus. But Jesus will always overcome evil," she says.

"I have never understood any of this, this way. It's all new to me," I say.

"Do you want to make that step right now? Do you want to tell Him you believe He died for you, personally?"

"Do I get struck by lightning if I say no?" I ask.

I don't know what I think. It's a lot to take in.

"Ha! No, I don't think you do," Piper says, laughing. "Some people like to read the Bible for themselves. You don't need me or a pastor or anything to talk to Him from your heart. It's a simple prayer of telling Him, you believe. God always knows when we are sincere. Tell Jesus you are sorry for your sins and that you want Him to come into your heart. The truth is, none of us know how long we have here on earth, so it's something to give real thought. The Bible also says that when anyone makes that decision, the angels have a big party in heaven."

"Then if I do it, what happens next?"

"You want to get to know Him better just like His twelve disciples did. Read your Bible, pray, go to church to meet other people who believe in Him. Start learning how to be His follower. It's a lifelong learning. No one ever 'arrives' and is done. We continue to grow and learn," Piper says.

"When did you make the choice?"

"It was after I came here. I met a dear nun down at St. Anne's— you know the church on the way to the other end of the island. I went there to see if I could get a job calling Bingo games and we developed a friendship, because we both loved watching the old black and white *I Love Lucy* shows. She's the one who had the conversation much like the one I am having with you," Piper says.

"A nun and *I Love Lucy*? That is quite a story," I say.

"I made the choice to give my life to Jesus, and it's never been the same. He gives me peace unlike anything I'd ever known before. Now, I pray about everything. Those nudges I was telling you about, He shows me what to do. We don't become perfect when we give our lives to Him, but we work on being like Him, because He is perfect. And when we mess up, and we all do, we simply sincerely tell Him we are sorry. It says in the Bible He puts our sins as far apart as the east is from the west. And He doesn't remember them anymore. We never have to be afraid to go to Him. He's not a harsh parent or big meanie waiting to catch us at something. He's loving. He doesn't condemn me; he lovingly shows me how to do better. He is love. As normal people, it takes a while to let that sink in. So, to answer your question, I made that choice five years ago!"

"Wow, I would think a lifetime because of how you talk about Him," I say.

"I have a long way to go. But He doesn't ask me to compare myself to anyone else. We are each so unique in His eyes. He loves us perfectly. No person on earth can love us as perfectly as Jesus loves us. What more could anyone ask for?"

"The nun, is she here? Do you go to church there sometimes?"

"It's a lovely church, but she is serving in a mission to help the poor in Africa. She comes back here on her time off. We love her dearly. That's the jar you gave money to, to hear Freddy's jokes," she says.

As the front door opens, I see Cam has arrived home.

"Listen Piper, I can't thank you enough for tonight. You have given me a lot to think about and I will. That Bible is going to move above the novel I'm reading on Hollywood wives. What a day," I say.

"Hi, ladies. Piper, I'm glad you got to have a friend over. I felt guilty about so many meetings this week, leaving you on your own," Cam says.

A friend. I could be her friend.

"We had a great time, and I feel like I know Gilda even more, which is a delight to me," Piper says.

"I'm going to head back. You two need a minute to yourselves," I say heading toward the door.

"Let me give you a hug," Piper says putting her arms around me.

"Really. Thank you. You've made more of a difference than you can imagine," I say.

"Call anytime, and if I don't see you sooner, I'll see you at class!" Piper says.

"Oh, I can't wait for that!" I say opening the door.

"I'll stand outside and watch you get on the porch. It's very safe here, but I don't take anything for granted," Cam says following me out the door.

He waves as I head through the dark toward the Grand. Slipping into the lower-level door once again, I know I can make it upstairs and elude the demitasse and coffee that happens after dinner every evening. The gentle music of the harpist is wafting through the air, and it adds to the calm feeling I have after spending time with Piper. Please be in our room,

Goldie, so we can make this horrible argument better. I don't hate you. I love you. You're my sister. I have so much to tell you.

Opening my door, it's quiet. She must still be out with Kris. As I turn on the light near the bed, I see a note. It has to be from her.

Dear Gilda,

Since I'm such a narca..narsi…so into myself, I won't bother you with my presence anymore.

The Grand had some openings so I took a room of my own, and I will pay for it myself. Don't try to find out where my room is. I need a break from you.

Let's not eat together for now, either. As far as I'm concerned, we are just two separate people staying here. I'm sorry if you have to eat alone, but I'll be dining with Kris from now on. He's not very high on you either.

Your "just-right" sister,

Goldie

P.S. For your information, he did just meet Katherine Sims-Dubois, and she was interested in him, just like I said.

Oh, what have I done? What have I done?

CHAPTER SEVENTEEN

When my sister said she wasn't talking to me anymore, she wasn't kidding. I suppose I could try to follow her and see what room she is staying in. Asking at the check-in desk didn't help. They keep people's room numbers private, and playing the sister card didn't work. She probably slipped the check-in staff some cash, so they wouldn't give me her room number. We've been here long enough, so they know who we are. I'm sure Goldie turned on the charm and made up a story, and they are all keeping quiet. She's being exactly like Granny who taught her staff to keep a tight lip. Plus, I'm no private detective or a Nancy Drew sleuth. This could be for the best. Let her cool off and we'll make up. We always do, although this may be one of the worst fights we ever had.

I'm so happy tonight is my art class at The Creative Lilac. Remi secured us a carriage to ride down together since it sounds like there may be rain in the forecast. That's nice. I wasn't too keen on walking home in the dark, and I bet it will be dark by the time we head back to the Grand. These fall days are different with the leaves turning, and the days are getting a little shorter.

Having time to myself has given me what I needed to look at

the Bible Piper gave me. I only read the first three chapters of John, but it does have me thinking. The problem is, I don't know what I'm *really* thinking. Am I gravitating toward this, because I'm having so many problems and when things calm down, I'll regret it? Still, if it's true, I'd be the foolish person Piper mentioned who doesn't get to see the truth behind all of it, if Jesus is who He says He is. It hurts my head. I'll give my brain a religion break for the rest of today and see what tomorrow brings. Today there will be art, art, and more art.

Managing to fritter away the day by doing nothing, I can't wait until I can head to Piper's class. Hmmm. No sightings of Goldie on the porch or at breakfast. I read where you can get meals brought up to your room. I bet that's what she is doing. Maybe she's having breakfast with Kris in her room and…, I can't even think of any possibilities there. I have to give her the benefit of the doubt that she knows what's right, and he is being a gentleman. Oh, brother, or should I say, oh sister. One more thing to worry about.

Finally, time to go! Piper said she would have all the supplies, but I can't help but bring the special watercolor journal I bought with the Round Island Lighthouse on the front. I want to do my island painting in this wonderful little watercolor book. When it comes to my journals and paper items in general, I love it all.

"Your carriage awaits, Mademoiselle Gilda," Remi says meeting me at the bottom of the stairs in front of the Grand Hotel.

"It is starting to rain, so good call on the carriage. Although, I don't think we would melt if we got a little wet," I say.

"Agreed. But why take ze chance?" Remi says with a twinkle in his eyes.

The familiar clip clop of the horses and the splash and sweet smell of rain makes me feel like I'm going to a magical place to do some of my favorite things. It's the calmest I've felt all week.

"I wonder how many people will be in this class. I know there are less people on ze island now than in the summer. I'm hoping we can each get some attention from Piper on how to use ze surfa…surfa…. what was that again? This is when my English can fail me," Remi says.

"The surfactant. I'm super excited to learn about this, too. There's so much I don't know, and I want to get better. I love learning new things, especially in art," I say.

Arriving in front of The Creative Lilac, Remi kindly opens and holds doors for me so I can grab my little satchel with my special book and pens. There's that lovely bell tinkle greeting us with what seems like a smile.

"Bonjour Freddy!" Remi says tipping his hat to him.

"Frere Jacques to you both, too!" Freddy says tipping back his imaginary hat.

Oh, he's a delight.

"Freddy, I see that's the extent of your French," I say.

"No, not so. I can say French fries and French toast. As you can see, I'm fluent in French!" Freddy says.

It feels good to laugh with happy people.

"We are here for ze class with Piper," Remi says.

"Yes, that will be upstairs, but before you go, may I invite you to once again revisit the little sign here at the register?" Freddy asks with an impish sweet smile.

"Of course you can. I wouldn't expect anything less from such a talent," I say dropping a few bills into his fundraiser jar.

"And what is your pleasure? Would you prefer me not to continue, or, and this would be my recommendation, would you prefer to hear something clever?" Freddy asks.

"Clever! Clever!" Remi and I both say at the same time.

"Clever it is, my friends. Since you were so generous with your giving Miss Gilda, I'm going to grace you with not just one, but two pearls of frivolity," Freddy says with a wink.

"Oh, I can't wait!" I say.

"One. Did you know there was a paddle sale at the boat store? Yes, indeed. It was quite an *oar* deal."

Remi and I both make sounds halfway between laughs and groans.

"Okay, you got us on that one," Remi says.

"And two. Even though there are no cars on the island, I do occasionally go over to the mainland and ride in a car. It had been so long, I couldn't work out how to fasten my seatbelt, but then in a few minutes, it just clicked!" Freddy says with his expectant look I've come to adore.

Remi and I laugh out loud. Not because it's that funny, but because every expression on Freddy's face is priceless.

"Well worth every penny, Freddy," I say.

"And you did such a good job, let me add to ze fund," Remi says, dropping a few bills into the jar.

"You are both so generous, and Sister Mary-Margaret's mission will be most grateful," Freddy says, patting the money jar.

I hear Piper's voice on the intercom next to the checkout area.

"Freddy, hopefully you've had enough time to fleece our guests, so would you send them on up, please?"

"Oh, Pip knows me so well," he says with a chuckle. "Head right on up the stairs my friends and enjoy your class. We will be closed by the time you are done, so I will bid you a grateful Frere Jacques until we meet again."

"Bye, Freddy. You enjoy your evening," I say heading toward the stairs.

"Yes, au revoir, dear friend," Remi says following me.

It's fun to hear Freddy lightly humming Frere Jacques as we climb the stairs to Piper's class.

"Welcome, friends! Welcome. I can't wait to dive into using surfactant with you," Piper says gesturing for us to sit at a round table.

"Are we early? Where are all the other students?" I ask.

"Funny story. Well, it's not funny I guess for my class size. I had several more students from friends, the Conrad family to fill out our table, so I closed the class to any more registrants. I keep the class size small, because I like everyone to get individual attention, especially with these products. At the last minute, they had relatives they hadn't seen in years coming to visit and had to bow out. So, it's just us three tonight," she says.

"More time with ze teacher. I am not complaining," Remi says.

"Sounds good to me, too," I say.

"Then, let's get started!" Piper says. "You'll notice you each have some ox gall liquid. We are going to use this to disrupt the water. And you will also see I have some gum arabic for you, which is the opposite and will give you some extra time by decreasing the drying time, so you can manipulate the blends and washes. And don't forget, it gives us the gloss we want for certain parts of our painting."

"I'm nervous, but excited!" I say.

"Remember, there are no mistakes, only opportunities to learn something new. That's the beauty of art. Rather than concentrate on getting a finished picture tonight, let's paint some shapes and then play with the surfactants, so you can see for yourself how they change a painting right in front of your eyes."

We both follow her instructions for painting some shapes in the colors of our choice and then add the magical new elixirs.

Piper smiles at each ohhh, and ahhh that neither of us can hold in as the colors take on new textures and dance on the paper.

We chit-chat like old friends as we learn. Now this is how to relax. These people and the watercolor are the perfect combination.

"Piper, I enjoyed ze sermon on Sunday. I'm sorry I didn't get to say hello to you and Cam. I ended up having an enjoyable conversation with ze pastor," Remi says.

"I'm sorry too, Remi. We had to get to our brunch appointment, so I had to leave," Piper says.

"Ze story of Mary and Martha tells us the importance of spending time with Jesus, that it's more important than busy work. For me, it made me think that I need to be about whatever ze Lord is bringing into my day as opposed to trying to get through my schedule. I can be extremely focused and miss people He may have put in my path," Remi says.

"I was so happy to see you there. I didn't realize when we first met that you were a fellow believer. That's wonderful. Have you been a Christian long?" Piper asks.

I don't know if I like where this conversation is going.

"No, not at all. I wish I would have known these truths when I was little, but I didn't know about Him until much older. I had a very scattered life in my past, and for many years I was an alcoholic. My next drink ruled my life. Being in Alcoholic Anonymous meetings pointed me to my higher power, and through some friends who introduced me to ze Bible, I knew that the higher power is God. I had been sober for a while, but it was only when I got down on my knees in my room and told Him, I was sorry for my life, and I wanted Him to be ze Lord from now on that my life really began. Since then, I read the Bible, pray to the Father, Son, and Holy Spirit, and go to church including any Bible studies I can find," he says.

"Oh, I have a Bible study here every week, but it's a lady's study. A bunch of gals got the flu, so we cancelled tonight. It's been my night for cancellations, but I don't mind. Like you, I like to follow what God is putting in my path, rather than my own plans. His ways are always better," she says.

"Always. When I quit drinking, I was finally able to work on some inventions that proved to be very successful and have provided me with ze means to live a good life in Canada. I had these ideas since I was a young man and visiting the U.S., but being a drunk, I could never follow through. If it wasn't for ze Lord giving me ze strength to stay sober and follow Him, I don't think ze rest of my story would be one to share," Remi says quietly.

"I'm so glad to hear the Lord delivered you from that life," Piper says. "He sure saved me from going down the wrong road I was headed, too."

"What did you think of the story of Mary and Martha, Gilda?" Remi asks.

I appreciate that Piper hasn't mentioned anything about our conversation at her place.

"It was very, um, enlightening. He was a good speaker, for sure," I say, dipping my head down, so they think I'm concentrating on my art.

"I have to say, I'm impressed by what you are both doing. The more you use these tools, the more you'll find ways to diversify your paintings," Piper says.

We paint a bit longer, and it's time for the class to be done. After friendly goodbyes, Remi and I enter the carriage that has come for us to head back to the Grand.

"It's nice the rain has stopped. Maybe we will see the stars tonight," I say. "I love the sound of these horses."

He doesn't say anything and when I look at him, I see he is intently staring at me.

"Are you okay, Remi?"

"I'm wondering, Gilda. Are you happy? Are you happy in ze life you are living?"

"Um. That's a hard question. Is it because I didn't talk a lot about religion?" I ask.

"No. Not at all. I simply want to know if you like your life, and if you are happy."

What should I say? *Am* I happy? Wait! What is *she* doing out now? Is she following me?

"Oh, no. Did you notice the lady we just passed on the side of the street in the swishy skirt walking the little white dog? She was under a streetlamp, and hard to miss."

"Possibly. My attention was much more on you," he says.

"Well, she noticed us. And, I can't exactly explain to you why, but when it comes to happiness, someone very influential in my life is going to be very unhappy if the person who just saw us gossips that I was out riding around in a carriage with a man, without Goldie," I say.

"Who is she?"

"She's the chairwoman of the town board, and she keeps her eye on everything happening, everywhere. Piper's shop is the only piece of property she doesn't own, and she's after Piper and Cam. We made it clear we like them when Goldie and I met her. Our meeting didn't go well. We are on her bad side," I say.

"I don't understand. You are now in danger?"

"Not so much in danger as in trouble with a relative. Listen, this is none of your concern. I'm probably overreacting. Goldie and I are on the outs, and it's messing with my mind. Forget I said anything. Let's just remember this wonderful evening learning new watercolor techniques," I say hoping he lets it go.

"Well, I do care about what happens to you. I won't do anything if you don't want me too, but I can pray for you. How about that? I will pray for you," Remi says as we exit the carriage back at the Grand. "Can I walk you to your room? It's on my way."

"No, thanks. I think I'm going to sit on the porch and see if I can see a star or two peek out from behind the clouds," I say.

"If you ever need anything, truly anything, know that I am here for you," Remi says leaning in and kissing me on the forehead.

"Thank you, Remi. Thanks for the carriage ride and being a great classmate," I say.

"Bonsoir, Gilda," Remi says heading inside.

Plopping down in one of the white wicker rocking chairs, I'm happy most of the guests have finished their demitasse in the parlor and moved on to the music in the Terrace Room.

More than one night I've ended my evening by sitting in the beautiful, cushioned area outside the Terrace Room watching the people head inside for drinks and dancing. I love hearing the tunes of Irving Berlin, Rodgers and Hammerstein, Cole Porter, Tommy Dorsey, Frank Sinatra, and Tony Bennet that wafts from the house band. I've also moved closer to the door to peek in and see the dancers brave enough to get out on the floor. They always look so happy to show off their various moves while others choose to sit and watch with a cocktail.

Tonight, I'm happy to sit here on the porch and breathe in the cooler evening air. I hope a star shows up so I can make a wish. Or maybe I should pray. Can I pray if I didn't tell Jesus I give Him my life yet? Am I allowed to talk to Him? Worth a try.

Forming words in my head while closing my eyes, all I can think of is, help me. Help me with Goldie. Help me with Granny. Help me with trying to understand if coming to You like a little child in faith is a fairy tale, or real.

"Well, seems *you* can have a romance but not me."

Opening my eyes, I know who it is.

"Goldie. You exist. Long time no see," I say.

I thought I would be happy to see her, but I feel mad all over again.

"So, you can have a boyfriend, who gives you a little kiss on the forehead, but I'm supposed to not be with anyone," she says.

"What are you talking about?"

"I saw Remi kiss you on the forehead. K-I-S-S-I-N-G!"

"Goldie, Remi is old enough to be an uncle or a father or whatever. I'm not having a romance with him. We had a very nice evening taking a watercolor class at Piper's, and that's all it was," I say.

"It's a thing. It's called an April- October fling or something like that," she says.

"You mean a May-December romance. No. That's not even close. He's a nice older man who has become a friend, and we love watercolor," I say. "Where's Kris?"

"He's inside. We left the dance floor for a moment to use the restrooms, and I stepped out here. I was on the other end of the porch when I caught you," she says.

"You didn't *catch* anything. It was a sweet gesture from a kind man. That's all it was. I haven't had one second of those kinds of thoughts for Remi, and I'm not happy to hear you even think that."

"Oh, but you can think anything you want about my boyfriend, and it's perfectly fine. Is that it?"

"Goldie, can't we *please* stop this fighting? You and I are the only people we have we can trust in this world. Let's agree to disagree and be done with it."

"Fine with me, but I'm not giving up my boyfriend. How do you feel about that?" Goldie asks. "By the way he doesn't like you."

"Kris doesn't like me?"

"Yes."

"How do you know that? He told you he doesn't like me?"

"Yes."

"Well, not everyone is going to like everyone."

And now he's here.

"There you are! Who likes who?" Kris asks.

"Nothing sweetie pie. It's sister stuff," Goldie says.

She's calling him sweetie pie now?

"Let's go dance some more, Kris. See yah, Gilda."

"Bye, Goldie. Don't be a stranger," I say, watching her walk off with him.

Watching them go, I see Kris turn and give me a look I don't like at all. I think I'm right. I don't trust him.

CHAPTER EIGHTEEN

Autumn on this island is magical. The leaves are bursting with crimson reds, tangerine orange, and luscious shades of yellow and maroon. No picture I've ever seen of fall scenes compare to seeing this place in person. The crisp air is perfect for a cozy sweater or sweatshirt.

Could I take a full winter here? Probably not. Granny usually plunks us in a warmer climate for the winter. From what I understand, most places here close by the end of October, including Grand Hotel. That means we don't have much longer before she'll be issuing some kind of edict about where we head next, if not back to her mansion.

I'm still not clear on why we ended up here except for Goldie's theory that she is in some kind of mafia life and simply needs us gone. I wonder if she's ever been here. Katherine Sims-Dubois said she had never met her, and with her nosy ways, I would think she would know if Granny did show up.

Anyone who has ever known Goldie or I before meeting Granny is always shocked when they meet her, especially because we call her Granny. I think they envision Granny on the *Beverly Hillbillies* in the old black-and-white TV show or an old lady sitting on the porch knitting. That's not our granny.

Granny tries to be like Dolly Parton, and she does a rather good job. Stylish boots and couture clothing. She's "fancy" as one of the maids once said. Granny has the money to hire the best doctors for facelifts or any lifts for that matter. She looks twenty years younger. She had our mom really young, and our mom had us really young. Granny is a fifty-something year old who looks way younger because of the lack of wrinkles.

Goldie and I used to go to our rooms and laugh our heads off anytime Granny would disappear for a day or two and come back with face bandages looking like the Mummy in the old movies. But then, after a while, a very unwrinkled, perfect Granny would emerge from her gauze cocoon and be ready to take on the world with her guns a blazing. Literally. Granny collects guns and practices at her on-site shooting range. I will say we always felt safe, as though if anyone tried to break in, Granny would take them out in a minute. She is an excellent shooter.

I wonder if Granny knows about John 3:16. About God loving the world and how we need to see that as something for ourselves. I'm starting to think it is real. I guess what I've been doing is praying. I am talking to God while I fall asleep each night. Goldie still insists on having her own room and keeping it a secret. I'm trying to respect her wishes.

It's been lonely doing most things by myself. It's been easier to skip breakfast in the dining room and eat in my room. I don't want to sit there and watch Goldie and Kris at a different table. It's too awkward. I'm glad Piper is stopping by today. She told me about a special place below the Grand most people miss called a labyrinth. She thinks I would love it and might even want to do some painting there.

Yikes! The morning has eluded me, and it's almost time to meet Piper on the porch.

Throwing on my favorite jeans and new sweatshirt with a lovely picture of Round Island Light house, I'm glad I'm getting to see Piper. I need someone to talk to. Jumping on the elevator,

I always wonder how full the lobby will be from day to day. The tourists come and go continually. As the door opens to the ding, there they are. A flurry of tourists enjoying this fantastic place scurrying through the parlor and out the front doors to the porch, exactly where I'm headed.

"Oh, I love your sweatshirt!" Piper says jumping up from one of the white wicker wonders as they have become known to me.

"Thank you. I just got it, and I love it, too. Did I keep you waiting?"

"No, not at all. I got here a few minutes early, and it felt great to sit down and let the sun hit my face."

"I know you have a busy day every day at your store, so taking time to show me the labyrinth…I hope I'm not imposing on your schedule," I say as we head down the stairs at the bottom of the Grand into the lovely yards that I see out my window every day.

"I love that you want to see this very special place. So, we head to these little woods you'll soon see. And of course, this pool we are passing is special, too. It was built in the 1920s and then renamed after Esther Williams, an actress and swimmer who filmed part of the movie, *This Time For Keeps*, here on the island," Piper says.

"There's a sign at the Grand about showing that movie next week. I'll have to try to catch it."

"Okay, here we are," she says pointing to words on a little sign at a small opening in the woods.

"So, it says it's about meditation," I say reading aloud.

"That's prayer really for the believer," she says.

"Walking a sacred path. Huh. It says it resembles a labyrinth constructed in the twelfth century at Chartres Cathedral in France. That is very interesting," I say.

Stepping through the opening, I see a circular path, almost like a maze that leads to a center. The maze is made up of plants and stones bordering the path.

"See, you stop here at the beginning on the outside, and you follow the path that winds its way around and around until you are in the center," Piper says. "Have you ever been in a labyrinth before?"

"No, this is my first time. So, praying in a circle?"

"Yes. You walk around and pray. I felt such peace the first time I came here. Then I would meet Cam here. This is one of the projects he takes personal control of, because it means so much to both of us. This is where we got married."

"Oh, my goodness. That's so beautiful!"

"It was a very small wedding with just us, the pastor, and Freddy. It will always be one of the most special moments in my life. In the summer, the flowers are much more prevalent in the circle, but now you see they are fading, and the colorful leaves have taken over. I think it adds to the beauty," Piper says with a tremble in her voice.

"I can see why you wanted me to see this place. It is so… well…peaceful. And I love how we are sheltered with the little woods…only this sweet little bench and the labyrinth here."

"And that bench is the perfect place to sit and sketch and do some painting with a travel paint set. The labyrinth is here for everyone, but most people have so much to see and are here for only a few days, they miss it. Selfishly, there's usually no one here which is why I love it. Especially now that the tourist season has calmed down a bit. You can really be here with your thoughts and your prayers," Piper says sitting down on the bench. "Go ahead, walk in the circle. I'm going to take a rest before I'm on my feet today."

Giving her a smile, I turn and put both of my feet at the beginning point and start to slowly walk. I hear a soft breeze rustling in the trees. With each step, I do feel something that could only be described as, well, sacred.

Jesus, is it possible for someone like me to know You? I have done so many terrible things in my life, can You forgive me? I do believe You died for me and took all my sins on the cross as it says in the Bible. I want to be Your child. I want to live the life Piper has talked about. Help me walk with You, just as I'm walking this path. Come into my heart. Help me know how to live with everything going on with my family. I trust You. Thank you, Jesus. Amen, I silently pray.

Somehow, I am here in the middle of the circle. With my head still bowing, I start back to the beginning of the circle. Glancing up, I see Piper with her head bowed as she sits on the bench. As I am reaching the end of the path, she looks up and our eyes meet. I see the tears in her eyes, and she sees the tears in mine.

"Do I sense that the angels in heaven are having a party right now?" she asks softly.

I gently nod and smile.

CHAPTER NINETEEN

*P*iper has been so kind to give me her time every morning for the past few weeks before she opens the store. We meet in her studio at seven am for an hour. She guides me through many stories in the Bible and what it means to be a Christian and serve Jesus. There's so much to learn and so many incredible stories! The Sermon on the Mount, The Lord's Prayer, The twenty-third Psalm, and the life of so many people in the Bible like Ruth, Esther, David, Paul, Isaiah.... all so strange to me. We pray, laugh, and cry.

I haven't shared all my story with her, and she doesn't push. She's so respectful. I spend my afternoons on my balcony with frequent trips to the labyrinth. I love it there. I feel sad I haven't seen Remi around. I'm trying to have feelings for Goldie that would please the Lord. That's a work in progress. The times I've seen her she makes a big deal about tossing her head in the other direction.

I'm still in bed here, because Piper couldn't meet this morning, and I think I'll go for a nice long walk today. The weather forecast calls for sun and sixty degrees. Perfect.

Crik. Crik.

Someone is opening my door, and I know I locked it.

"Get up, get up! I waited to see if you were finally going to show up at breakfast for a change, but you didn't!"

"Goldie! You scared me to death. I forgot you still have the key to this room."

"Of course. Why would I give that up?"

"Well, it must be something big for you to show up after not speaking to me very much the past few weeks. What happened? Did Kris leave, and now you're willing to be friends again?"

"Oh, don't be a grouch. Look at this!"

Oh joy, another telegram. Here comes the stomachache. Telegrams only mean one thing.

"*Will be there in time for dinner. Stop. Have reserved the small private dining room on the side for us. Stop. Please be there at six pm sharp. Stop. I look forward to seeing my girls. Stop. We have much to discuss. Stop,*" I say reading the message out loud.

"What is the deal? Not a peep for weeks, and now she will be here tonight. How does she even know there is a side room to reserve?" Goldie asks, grabbing the telegram from my hand and staring at it.

"Why are you so hyped up? We didn't do anything wrong," I say.

"What's the whole 'we have much to discuss' mean? That can't be good," she says.

"It might not be anything. You know the Grand is going to close for the season soon, and we have to go somewhere. I do agree it's strange she is coming here instead of us just going home or being shipped somewhere else. Still, we shouldn't assume the worst," I say.

"That doesn't sound like you. You always assume the worst."

Help me, Jesus. She knows how to push my buttons.

"Something happened to me a recently. I gave my heart to Jesus," I say waiting for a reaction.

"What? Getting all religious? Are you going to become a nun, now?"

"No. Piper told me about a verse in the Bible, and I memorized it. John 3:16. *God so loved the world He gave His only Son that whoever believes in Him would not perish but have everlasting life.* She told me to put my name in there…instead of whoever. That He died for me to forgive me of my sins. I agreed with what I learned. I am a sinner and needed Him to save me. You could do the same thing, too."

"I knew it was a mistake to leave you alone so much. You've gone off the deep end. You're just doing this so Piper will like you more. This is her fault," Goldie says.

"No Goldie. This is something that's very real and important. I didn't make the decision lightly. I know it's right. It's right for you, too," I say.

"Once again, you think you know what's right for me. Maybe I'll become an atheist and then tell you I know that's right for you. Would that make you jump on the bandwagon? Oh, look at Saint Gilda. Now when we get in a car on the way home, you'll have to ride on the dashboard."

Clearly this isn't the time to be talking to her about Jesus.

"Let's not fight. We have to be united tonight when Granny comes, or she's going to make both of our lives worse. You know our unity is the only thing that has ever held her back," I say.

"I can agree with you on that. I wonder if she would mind if Kris came to the dinner?"

"I wouldn't bring him if I were you. I'm sure there is time to introduce him later. Besides, I bet he has no desire to sit and hear any family business of any kind."

"I guess you're right. And who knows what mood Granny will be in. There may be yelling. I hope that the side room is soundproof," Goldie says.

I hope so, too, sister. I hope so, too.

CHAPTER TWENTY

"Okay, I'm ready too. Head to my room and give a quick knock. We can walk down to dinner together. Did you see any signs of Granny or any of her people around this afternoon?" I ask Goldie on the phone.

"I wasn't out much, but when I was, no I didn't see anyone. I couldn't find Kris today either, so I didn't feel so bad about not having dinner with him tonight. This is all feeling a bit creepy, isn't it?"

"Creepy, surreal, disturbing. Don't you think it's odd that we haven't seen our grandmother who has been like a mother to us our whole lives, and neither of us are excited to see her? Instead, we are using those words to describe being with her again. That's not right," I say.

"I guess not. But for us, it's normal. Dreading Granny's big reunion meetings are just part of our lives. As long as the money flows into my bank account, I can always choose to ignore the rest," she says.

"Okay. I'll wait for your knock," I say.

"Be there in a sec."

Hanging up the phone the weight of my words hits me. It should feel good to see your family. Instead, I'm filled with fear and dread. I'll have to see later if there's anything in the Bible about that. Taking one last look in the mirror, I guess I look okay. Granny will find fault about something, so once again I'm trying to please this impossible to please person.

Knock, knock.

Opening the door, I see Goldie has put her best foot forward with perfect hair, makeup, and dress. Entering the elevator, I feel queasy. Lord, help me. From what I've come to understand, You are with me always. Help me now. I wish I had time to ask Piper to pray for me, but she wasn't available when I called. So, it's You and me Lord. Help.

CHAPTER TWENTY-ONE

*L*ike a queen holding court, Granny sits at the far end of the room at the head of the table. I've never eaten in this private dining area off the main dining hall, but with Granny involved, I'm thankful we won't be eating with a large group of people. I knew she'd either be here early to set the tone or arrive with a grand entrance. Since there isn't anyone to impress, set the tone it is.

"Hello, girls. Wonderful to see my young ladies. Come give Granny a hug," she says.

"Hello Granny," I say.

"Hi Granny," Goldie says as we both make our way toward her.

With a light pat for a second from each of us, the fake hugging is over. That's all the niceties we can probably expect for this evening. The door opens, and of course, Granny would bring her faithful companion.

"Say hello to Jeeves. He's accompanied me on this trip," she says nodding to Jeeves who takes a seat near the door.

"Hi Jeeves, nice to see you," we say almost in unison.

"Ladies," Jeeves says with a nod toward us. His demeanor

around Granny is always different from when we get to talk to him alone. This is buttoned-up, rigid Jeeves. Not our favorite.

"As you see, I've asked the staff to set up this lovely buffet, so we could talk while you dine. Help yourself. I've already eaten, and it's quite delicious," Granny says sipping coffee.

Filling up our plates we give each other a sideways glance, because here comes the other shoe dropping that we've been expecting since we arrived.

"There now. Enjoy your meal. Have you ladies been behaving yourselves on this island?" Granny asks, looking first at me.

She's wearing one of her blonde shag-type wigs she copied after seeing Dolly Parton on TV. Somehow, she even found out where Dolly gets her wigs and started ordering hers from the same source. Sure, the house staff won't tell us anything about our mother, but this tidbit, they didn't mind passing on. A red suit with her signature shoulder pads, wide belt, and chunky necklace are typical for her "I mean business" look she sports when she is going to a meeting. That doesn't bode well for us.

"We've had a wonderful time. We have never known quite why we are here, but the island is a magical, beautiful place," I say feeling like Dorothy talking to the wizard when he's behind the curtain in Oz. Why does this woman intimidate me so much?

"You look a little pale, Gilda. Perhaps a bit more blush next time?" Granny says. Of course. Find something wrong.

"I told her, more blush. I wanted to teach her the technique to get it just right, but she won't listen," Goldie says.

Goldie, please. Remember our unified front here!

"And you Goldie? Meet anyone special?" Granny asks.

"Why are you asking me that?" Goldie says.

"Just polite conversation. You are the one of my girls who tends to look for that someone special wherever you go. With the amount of time, you've been here, I can only assume you would have a special friend by now," Granny says.

With a sideways glance at Goldie, I'm not sure what she's going to say.

"No. No one special. I've made friends, sure. But they are all casual acquaintances that come and go. Most people aren't staying here as long as we are. Speaking of which, the place is going to close soon Granny. We'd like to go home," Goldie says.

Goldie's look is telling me in sister language; *don't say anything.*

"I wanted to get together with you girls to tell you about my future plans for you," Granny says opening a leather portfolio.

"Plans? We wanted to go home…" I say.

"Yes, I heard. But that's not what is happening. I think it's time you girls got more of a purpose in your life. Most people don't get to go from place to place and live in the lap of luxury without any responsibilities," she says.

"We tried to do something constructive, but you made sure it failed," I say.

"Spending your college years drinking more than studying is something I made happen?" she asks, with her voice rising.

"No. That was our choice. But we tried to get jobs, and you sabotaged us," Goldie says.

"That's your version of what happened and highly unlikely. I have more going on in my life and business to attend to, with little care to 'sabotage' young ladies who fully rely on my money to support them," she says lowering her voice again, regaining control. "That being said, I wasn't perhaps as supportive as I could have been. That's why this time; we will work together to move you forward in life."

"What if we don't like your plan?" I ask.

"You have always been free to move on. You are both of legal age. If you choose to go out into the world on your own, which includes supporting yourselves, I will not stop you," she says with a tone that has taken on a fake sweetness that makes my heart pound.

Her voice reminds me of when Piper and I studied the

snake talking to Adam and Eve in the Garden of Eden. I imagined this same syrupy hiss.

"I'm sure whatever Granny has for us will be wonderful. We don't need to be talking about messing with our bank accounts. Come on, Gilda. Give Granny a chance. You are being very rude," Goldie snaps at me.

When it comes to keeping her money, Goldie has no problem throwing me under the bus.

"I have planned for you both to move into a nice apartment in San Diego, California. The weather there is lovely. I've enrolled you both in a business school, so you can learn the basics of taxes and commerce. Then, depending on how you do, you can both eventually join my business that your grandfather began. I want to make plans for the family legacy to continue for many years to come," she says with a satisfied smile.

"But, Granny, I can barely add and subtract. My love is art, not taxes and numbers!" I say.

"You took aptitude tests while you were in high school. You both showed high ability to master math and logic so that's what you should be doing. If you want to paint in your free time, I don't care. But your main obligation will be learning business and tax laws," Granny says.

"Oh, so we can work around taxes with all your mafia money?" I say.

Goldie just audibly gasped, and I've never seen her eyes wider. I can't believe what I just said either, but I'm not doing this anymore.

"What did you say to me?" Granny asks standing up and glaring at me.

"Ask Goldie. She thinks you are in the mafia and that all the people we've seen through the years are thugs who work for you," I say blurting it out quickly before I lose my nerve.

"You both know I have a business from the patent your grandfather had," she says.

"Yes, but then you take those profits, and I don't know how, but you use the money illegally to invest in shady businesses off the books. That's where you make your real money," I say, standing up myself.

"You better watch yourself, young lady," Granny says.

"I don't hear you denying it. If you think I'm going to some business school and then going into business with you to cook your books, you're crazy," I say.

"It was a joke! When I said Granny was in the mafia, it was a joke, Gilda! I don't believe she is really in the mafia," Goldie says. "Everyone sit down and calm down. You know Granny has always only had the best in mind for us. Right, Granny?"

"Well, I'm glad at least one of my granddaughters still has some sense. I've never heard of such a preposterous theory," Granny says, sitting down.

"What happens if we don't follow your plan?" I ask.

"Then you're on your own. Your money stops. Both of your bank accounts are also in my name. I have full control of your money," she says.

"I don't believe you," I say. "There is something shady going on, and I don't want to be a part of it."

"Oh, did I mention that this is a sister deal? You both comply, or you both get cut off," she says with a sense of satisfaction in her voice.

"What? No! If Gilda won't go to the school ,and I will, then we are both cut off?" Goldie asks.

"You heard me," Granny says. "Oh, and something else. I'm not putting up with lies anymore from either of you. I need to know I can trust you."

"We didn't lie about anything," I say.

"Jeeves, would you invite our guests in, please?" Granny says gesturing to Jeeves.

Standing and opening the door, Jeeves waves his hand for someone to come in.

"Hello Katherine. Hello Vincent," Granny says motioning to the open chairs.

Katherine swishes to a seat with an air of arrogance. I want to slap her in the face. I knew she was a spy.

"Vincent? That's not Vincent! That's Kris!" Goldie says.

"Let's revisit the conversation on lies," Granny says.

This nightmare just keeps getting worse. Oh, Lord help us!

CHAPTER TWENTY-TWO

"Kris, what's going on?" Goldie says, turning to him.

"Goldie, my real name is Vincent. I'm sorry. I was really starting to like you, but hey, a buck's a buck, you know?"

The debonair tone he's used around us suddenly sounds much flatter.

"I thought you never knew Granny, Katherine? Seems *you* are the liar!" I say.

"I wasn't lying. I had never met her until earlier today. Did we correspond? Yes. But I never met her in person," Katherine says crossing her legs to reveal another hideous pair of pumps with daisies painted on the tips. Ugh. What a way to ruin my favorite flower. It should be a painting of bats or snakes.

"Katherine is what she said she was. An acquaintance of an acquaintance who was willing to help me for a generous donation to her causes. When she let me know that Goldie was suddenly partial to redheads—and I've always noticed how she is enamored around professional athletes—Katherine was able to supply a distant cousin who had a flair for acting and a love of money. Having Vincent show up on the island was her brilliant idea," Granny says with a nod to Katherine.

"What is the point of that? Why did Goldie liking redheads have anything to do with this?" I ask.

"Two-fold. First, she thought maybe he could be helpful in weaseling into your friendship with Cam and Piper, helping her get that property she wants," Granny says.

"Unfortunately, that didn't happen. I didn't know Cam was such a football fan. Turns out, Vincent knows very little about football," Katherine says looking at him with a frown, and speaking in the weird way she does with all her words flowing together and not pausing.

"How was I supposed to know? I never played sports," Vincent says. "I only did the football story as a kicker for the Packers, because the team was close, and I thought it was something Goldie might find exciting. It was the backstory I picked for myself. I thought it was rather clever."

"The point is, when you take an acting job, study up! You must do better," Katherine says, dropping the r at the end of better so it sounds more like 'betta.'

"Hey, I did a lot for this job. I'm not a redhead and getting that dye job so quickly was no easy task. You could have let me know Cam liked football. I tried to sound like I knew what I was talking about," Vincent says. "At least I got us all together by jumping on that chance to go to that church and have lunch."

"Yes, exactly what you *shouldn't* have done, because he had too much time to talk to you about football." Katherine says.

"I'm sorry that the plan didn't work for you Katherine, but it worked perfectly for me. Now I know my girls can easily lie to me. I'm extremely disappointed about that," Granny says.

"So, everything we had wasn't true, Kris? Or I guess it's Vincent?" Goldie asks with a tear in her eye. "You're not even a redhead?"

"Nope, I'm a blonde. Listen, babe. I enjoyed every minute with you. I did. Uh, it seems I learned you can tell a nice little lie yourself. Writing a book on islands, huh? Not true as I've come to understand. This was just another job for me. You are gorgeous, but I'm partial to brunettes," Vincent says coldly.

"You jerk! Such a low life. And you, too, Katherine," I say.

"That will be enough of that, Gilda," Granny says. "I won't tolerate you being rude to our guests. Thank you, both. Probably best you leave now."

"It was a pleasure to help you out. I'm glad you are satisfied you got what you wanted. Keep in touch. I feel like we could do some remarkable things in the future," Katherine says. "Come along Vincent. I have your ferry ticket, and it's time for you to head home."

"You have to admit, I was rather good at being Kris Topher. What a name. Like anyone would ever have that name! See yah, Goldie. No hard feelings I hope," Kris says leaving along with the swish swish of Katherine's skirt.

At least I know I was right about both of them. Totally untrustworthy.

"You know, Katherine, you talk funny," Vincent says.

"Shut up, Vincent." I hear her saying as she leaves.

"So, girls. You have some decisions to make. I think it's clear what would be in your best interest. Close the door would you, Jeeves? Now let's get down to more details…"

As Jeeves is closing the door, it's pushed back open.

"Bonjour, Madame Locks. Long time, no see."

Remi Chapeau. Why is Remi here?

CHAPTER TWENTY-THREE

"What are *you* doing here?" Granny asks, rising again. "How did you—"

"Surprised to see me, Katrina? I guess your plan to keep me away didn't work," Remi says approaching us at the table.

"Remi, you know Granny?" I ask.

"We have a long history that goes way back," he says staring intently at her.

"But then, you knew who I was before we met?" I ask. I'm so confused.

"Of course he did. Seems you were deceived by a liar. Now you know why I can't stand lying so much," Granny says.

"Please, Katrina. You've lied so much in your life, you don't even know ze truth anymore," Remi says. "Gilda, please withhold your judgement until you hear ze whole story. I had a very good reason I didn't tell you who I was at first. I would have told you much sooner, but you may have noticed I have been gone for a little while. That's thanks to Katrina, or Granny as you call her."

"I can't believe everything I'm hearing. Are Gilda and I the only ones who have no idea what's going on around here?" Goldie asks.

"Remi, I could have you removed again. Jeeves, show him out," Granny says.

"Not this time, Katrina. I only had one of my people with me when you ambushed me, but this time, I have far more than you do," Remi says staying put.

Granny squints, stamps her feet, and gives him a stare. She must think he's telling the truth, because she sits back down and motions Jeeves to do the same.

"You sent me on a wild goose chase with a deceptive telegram, and then tried to detain me over ze Canadian border until my people figured it out. I can imagine your plan was to keep me there until you had made sure Gilda and Goldie left once again, making it hard for me to find them," Remi says. "Ze reason I couldn't tell you earlier ladies was, because I have been trying to figure out if you are happy in ze lives you have."

That's why I haven't seen Remi around. It was Granny's doing!

"For many years, I did not pursue ze truth of what I am about to tell you. I had a drinking problem, just as my brother did so many years ago." Remi says.

"This is all preposterous. Lies. Fabrications..." Granny says with the volume in her voice growing once again.

"What does this have to do with us?" I ask.

"Ze truth is Gilda, I am your uncle. Your father was my brother!" Remi says.

"Our uncle? You knew our father? We've always wanted to know more about him," Goldie says.

"No, not *your* uncle, Goldie. I am so sorry to tell you this truth, but you and Gilda are not twins. You are not even blood relatives," Remi says gently.

No! I can't believe what I'm hearing! My sister is *not* my sister? How can this be?

"What are you talking about Remi? This isn't making any sense!" I say. I think I'm going to pass out. My stomach is lurching. My head is woozy.

"You must both know ze truth, finally," Remi says.

"What are you doing? Trying to split up sisters? Trying to split up my family?" Granny screams.

"Sit down, Katrina," Remi says firmly.

Two big men open the door and look at Remi.

"We are fine gentlemen, but please, stay close outside. I'll call you if I need you," Remi says as they nod and leave the room.

"You're a liar! You have concocted some weird theory, and I'm not going to sit here and listen to your dribble anymore. Let's get out of here, girls. I'll protect you from this monster," Granny says standing.

"He's telling you the truth."

I can't believe my ears. Jeeves is speaking up!

CHAPTER TWENTY-FOUR

"Shut up, Jeeves. You'll shut up if you know what's good for you!" Granny says glaring at him.

"This is going to happen, Katrina. Ze truth is coming out finally, so you might as well face it. Sit down or I'll call my men in here," Remi says. "Then you can get ze same treatment you gave me."

"Whatever he says, girls, don't believe him!" Granny says sitting down.

"Here's ze truth. Ze real story. Most of these facts have taken much investigative work to uncover, but it is ze truth," Remi says with emphasis on the word truth. "When we were young men, my brother and I left Canada together to play in a band in the U.S. for a four-month tour. We knew it was risky, because there was little money promised, but we were young, stupid, and had no jobs or money— nothing to keep us in Canada."

"Of course, like most musicians, we thought we were going to be ze next Rolling Stones. At our first gig, we met Gilda's mother. She and her friend told us they had snuck out to see our band play. My brother and Gilda's mother, Lisa, hit it off immediately. I barely saw him at that stop because they were together all the time. Young love, you know? My brother told Lisa ze rest of ze towns and venues we were playing in on our tour."

"When we arrived at ze next venue, there would usually be a letter for my brother from Lisa. Then, after playing all those mostly dive bars, ze tour was over. We had nothing new booked and barely enough money to survive. While we were at ze last gig, Lisa's letter arrived telling my brother we should come and stay with her at her friend's place. That's where she was living. That friend was Patty Locks, your mother Goldie," Remi says.

"Rubbish. Don't listen to any of this, girls," Granny says.

"It's my time to have ze floor. Be quiet, Katrina," Remi says. "I have waited years for this moment, and you are going to listen."

I hear Granny muttering under her breath with words no one would repeat in church.

"So, if this is all true, my mother was Lisa…" I say.

"And, my mother was Patty," Goldie says, finishing my thought. "Granny, you always said our mother's name was Sophia."

"Her name *was* Sophia. You think this lunatic knows the name of my own daughter more than I do? He's an evil liar!" Granny says.

"That name, Sophia, was made up to make sure it would be harder to trace her, I'm sure," Remi says. "Her name *was* Patty."

"You're right. Any time we thought about trying to learn more about our mother, there were threats to disown us, because we were ungrateful. After a while, we quit trying," I say, looking at Granny who is staring away and not looking at me or Goldie.

"Remember, they were girls in their late teens. Neither of them were married. Right after they had snuck into town to see us, Katrina found out. Some snitch she probably paid in town saw them at ze concert and tipped her off. That's when your grandparents sequestered them and didn't let them go anywhere. From what I've learned, Katrina paid little attention to Patty growing up, leaving most of ze care to hired help," Remi says. "Once she was a teenager and didn't need someone to watch her all ze time and especially once Lisa moved in, Katrina wasn't paying much attention at all. That's how ze girls were originally able to sneak around more, until Katrina caught wind of what was happening."

"Our poor mothers," I say. "Didn't they go to school?"

"Patty was tutored at home. Lisa was an orphan who, once she turned sixteen, figured out how to elude the foster care system. By the time Katrina noticed Patty's friend hardly ever left, Patty threatened all kinds of things if Lisa couldn't stay. So, they let her stay and gave her household chores like a maid to pay for her room and board. I think I remember Lisa saying they originally met the first time Patty snuck out of the house. They became instant friends. With no family and nowhere to go, Lisa stayed with Patty," Remi says.

Hmmm. If this is true, her parenting style hasn't changed much. Sounds like they were raised just like us, by staff.

"You see, they didn't yet live in ze place you girls remember as ze house where you grew up. That mansion came after ze money started to pour in. They were still rich by most standards, especially in ze little town where they lived, but not wealthy like Katrinia is now. At that time, they lived far from town, out in the country on winding roads in a large forest," Remi says.

"I thought we had lived in our mansion for many generations. That's what I always heard," Goldie says.

"Listen here…" Granny says standing again.

Remi barks at her to stay seated and threatens to call in the men standing outside the door. I can't believe it; she sits back down. I've never seen Granny listen to anyone.

"I will continue," Remi says giving her a dirty look. "So, my brother and I decide to show up at this place in the middle of nowhere to see ze girls. We hitchhiked there, which everyone did in those days. What we didn't know when we decided to visit was that your mothers were both pregnant! At first, Katrina was furious that we showed up. After ze girls begged, she agreed to let us stay in the carriage house in the back of their property for one night."

"Ze girls denied that we had anything to do with them being pregnant and insisted we were merely friends, but Lisa knew my brother was indeed ze father of her baby. She didn't want Katrina to know. Patty told us she had no idea who could be her baby's father. They were very promiscuous times. Eventually, Lisa told my brother she was sure he was ze father of her baby. But I'm getting ahead of myself. With no money and no plans, we were happy to stay for ze night and then be on our way."

I'm so blown away I can't speak. From Goldie's expression, she must be feeling the same way. Granny won't stop muttering under her breath.

"Ze next morning, Katrina's demeanor had completely changed. She was nice to us. It was very hard to understand. She told us if we wanted to help around their house, she would let us stay in the carriage house a while longer. We could do yard work, drive their car if they needed a chauffeur, and do odd jobs. In exchange, she would provide us with food and lodging. It all sounded good to us, because she also let us have access to her liquor cabinet. Ze girls were happy, because they had friends again after being stuck out there for ze past few months. What we didn't know was, Katrina, as usual, had ulterior motives," Remi says.

"I don't know if all this is even possible," Goldie says.

"It all happened, Goldie. This is what I have been able to piece together after much, much research," Remi says.

"You sound like you're on some kind of drugs. Are you high on cocaine? Is that why you have us stuck here telling us these ridiculous stories?" Granny says.

"I've pieced it all together, Katrina, like an intricate puzzle. You and I both know your plan was to try and convince us to marry Patty and Lisa to save face from having pregnant teens under your roof. Don't think for one minute, girls, it was out of care for her daughter, Patty. Even if ze girls had married us, she would have figured a way to get us out of ze picture eventually, I'm sure," Remi says.

"Our mothers were pregnant. Didn't they have to go to the doctors in town?" I ask.

"Oh no. Katrina always thought of every detail. A doctor came to ze home for check-ups, and it was arranged for home births. Ze doctor would come to the house to deliver ze babies. She made sure no one outside of her influence would know what was going on with ze girls. She bribed and blackmailed her way to get what she wanted in any circumstance. No one would dare cross her, as my brother and I soon came to understand as well," Remi says.

"Keep talking, Remi. The more you talk, the more time I have to think up what is going to come your way when I leave this room," Granny says with a sneer.

Remi gives her a dirty look before continuing.

"Katrina thought ze girls would jump at the chance to marry us, but they both refused. They said they would not marry under these circumstances. My brother and I did not have money and were still drinking heavily. We were highly irresponsible. Your grandparents weren't very happy once they realized their plan wasn't going to work. To her credit, even though Lisa liked my brother very much, she was smart enough not to accept marriage after she saw how we both behaved. We spent part of every day getting drunk. Once that plan failed, you would think your grandparents would have kicked us out, but they didn't. After a surly few days, Katrina once again became even nicer to us. We couldn't understand it."

"This unbelievable escapade you are making up gets more bizarre by the minute," Granny says. "No one is believing a word you are saying."

Ignoring her this time, Remi keeps talking.

"Here's *why* she kept us around. While we were there, your grandfather would stop out to ze carriage house for a drink. My brother and I would often draw up sketches of a plan we had to possibly revolutionize the lifespan of batteries. Think about it. Batteries are in everything. If we could bring this to pass, ze possibilities were endless. Yes, we were young and stupid, but we were also gifted in music and in electronics...we were always thinking up new inventions. Your grandfather, with his technical background, recognized that our ideas were both technically sound and amazing."

"He told Katrina, and that's why she kept us there. She was weaseling her way to steal those plans from us and take them for herself. We had no idea how to make something work past ze invention stage, but she and your grandfather had the resources and connections to bring these ideas to life! Of course, we didn't realize what they were doing at the time. And Katrina always made sure we had plenty of alcohol, another way of controlling us."

"There, you see. He admits he has an alcohol and drug problem," Granny says.

"Why did you stay? There wasn't a future for you there. Why didn't you go back to Canada?" I ask.

"Because we had a roof over our heads and food to eat. And, and we liked to hang out with ze girls," Remi says. "Even though they didn't want to marry us, they still liked being with us. When my brother did eventually find out he was ze father of Lisa's baby, he thought she might change her mind and be with him. He had hopes of being a real father to their baby. That's you, Gilda."

"A real family," I say quietly not wanting Goldie to hear.

"Your father wanted to be a part of your life, Gilda," Remi says.

"What was my father's name?"

"Phillipe. Phillipe Chapeau," Remi says.

"Can I meet him? Will you take me to meet him?" I ask.

"Hold on sweet girl, there is more to the story. So, we stayed. We had no idea of Katrina's real intentions," Remi says.

I've never seen the look of astonishment Goldie has on her face. It must match the look on my face. And that's not even the whole story?

"At first, I didn't know any of this. It wasn't until I went to Alcoholics Anonymous a little later in my life and became sober, ze pieces of this tragic puzzle started to come together and make sense. I also learned there was a God who loved me and sent His Son to die for me. I became a Christian, and I asked God to help me find my niece and right this wrong. I have had to be very patient to get to this day, but I praise God it is finally here!" Remi says.

"Oh, now God is with you? I highly doubt that. God doesn't like fakes and liars," Granny says snidely.

"I will continue Katrina! When I recovered and could think about more than where my next drink was coming from, I began to reconstruct ze plan my brother and I had for ze new type of battery while adding in even more ideas from ze technology of this day and time. Even though I figured out she had stolen our plans, gotten her own patent, and taken control of it in the U.S, she did not have ze patent in Canada or Europe. This was a big oversight on her part. That's probably because, as I discovered, she was investing her time in illegal activities to make vast amounts of money in a seedy world no moral businessperson would ever be involved in. That's where she put her efforts."

Standing up, Granny starts to make a loud, slow clap.

"The biggest amount of hogwash I have ever heard! You expect these highly intelligent young ladies to believe a word of this?" Granny says. "Girls, he's obviously graduated from the bottle to hard drugs, because he's high as a kite."

"Sit down, Katrina. I have spent thousands upon thousands of dollars and hired every resource I could to come to this day. I will tell ze whole story," Remi says sternly.

"Oh, yes. Please do. It keeps getting better by the minute. Take it all in girls, because this is going to give us all a huge laugh when we ditch this psychopath," Granny says plopping down in her chair.

"Here is more of why I didn't come for you right away, Gilda. Shortly after you were both born at home within days of each other, Katrina arranged with ze owner of a local store that carried baby items to stay open for a private shopping trip after the store had closed. I'm sure she bribed people to do what she wanted, like opening a store just for them and then making sure they kept quiet about her daughter buying baby items. Patty said she wouldn't go unless Lisa and my brother could come and get some things, too. I was tasked with driving everyone there. Patty and Lisa had become as close as sisters, and Granny knew she had better not mess with Lisa, or she would lose Patty, and now her new granddaughter. So, off we went to ze store— all of us. Your grandparents, me, my brother, Lisa, and Patty. Ze babies stayed behind with ze help," Remi says, pausing to take a drink of water and I notice his hands are shaking.

"I think I know what's coming," I say.

"Yes, partially. But not all of it," Remi says.

I hear Granny make a snorting sound under her breath, and Remi glares at her again.

"It was a very rainy night. Ze rain was coming down in sheets so dense, it was hard to see ze road," Remi's voice starts to tremble. "I was driving as slow as I could. I hadn't gone far and even asked about turning back, but Katrina insisted we go to ze store. Ze last thing I remembered was losing control and veering toward large trees. I lost consciousness at that point. When I woke up, we were back at ze house. Big men were scrambling around. I asked what was happening and Katrina told me, I had killed everyone in the car except her and myself!" Remi says choking out the last sentence through tears.

Gasping in unison, Goldie and I are both crying. Granny has no expression on her face at all. This woman has ice water in her veins!

"I'm so sorry girls. This is why you were both babies with no mothers who ended up being raised by your grandmother. Once ze accident happened, Katrina took over ze situation to make it look exactly as she wanted. That is what she always did and always does. Right after the accident, Katrina had her thugs move ze body of her husband—your grandfather—into the house. She did ze same with her daughter, Patty. She obviously had ze coroner in her back pocket, too, because it was made to look like your grandfather died of a heart attack. She further covered up the story by saying her daughter Patty had given birth to twins and had died in childbirth. That's the story she wanted the world to know and only staff knew what really happened that night. To the rest of the world, Lisa and my brother Phillipe never existed. She disposed of the car and their bodies so there would never be a trace of them. Lisa had no family to inquire about her, and well, you know how she handled me ever saying anything about Phillipe. Why Katrina decided to keep you both, that is for her to say. I imagine it was easier than trying to figure out what to do with another baby in the home," Remi says.

"You will pay for all these lies, Remi. You will pay," Granny says in a voice that is almost a hiss.

"Yes, I feared you for years Katrina, but not anymore. Ze truth is—ze crumpled car with my brother and Lisa inside was never seen again. We were in ze middle of nowhere and ze accident happened near ze house, so this was all possible for her to pull off. She took care of me right away, too. While I was unconscious she had me brought into the house, too. I was still very woozy and did not fully comprehend what had happened. Very shortly, immigration officers were at the door taking me to deportation, because my visa had expired. In hindsight, I was not only woozy from the accident, but Katrina made sure there were drugs in my system. No one would listen to anything I was saying. All they saw was a young man who appeared to have a drug and alcohol problem, not to mention, now illegally in ze country. And as always, anything that wasn't legal, Katrina took care of with pay offs and bribes," Remi says.

"It's all so heartbreaking," I say. I can't wrap my head around so much evil.

"And I am so sorry to tell you all this, but you are now adults, and you must know," Remi says.

"None of this is true my darling girls. None of it," Granny says having recovered a sickly-sweet tone to her voice.

"Katrina also said, if I ever did try to come after her, or try to take Gilda, it would not go well for you, Gilda," Remi says looking at Granny.

"I am going to sue you to kingdom come for all these lies," Granny says. "Girls! You're going to take the word of a drug addled, liar with no proof for any of this over me, who raised you, cared for you, and has supported you both for twenty-two years?"

"What reason would he have to come and tell this story if it weren't true, Granny?" I ask. "I know Katherine saw Remi and I in the carriage together, so she told you there was a man here. Somehow you figured out it was Remi. Then you sent a telegram to get him within your grips, and you had your thugs detain him. You must have known he was going to tell this story soon, and you were hoping to have Goldie and I gone before he got back."

"More delusional talk. I'll tell you why he has come here with this ridiculous story. Money! He wants more money and the US battery patent. He wants to say it wasn't your grandfather's patent and that it was his. He wants all the money that made us so rich. Can't you see that? It's always, all about money!" Granny says.

"It explains why Goldie looks like you, and why I don't. Outside of the blonde hair, which is only that color because you insist I dye it, I look nothing like your family," I say. "I was only blonde when I was very little."

"That means nothing. Haven't you met people before who look nothing like their family?" Granny asks.

"I have. That's true," Goldie says.

"As to ze question as to why I didn't come for you sooner, Gilda, as I mentioned before, Katrina went to ze extent of having her thugs keep an eye on me through ze earlier years. She even paid people to befriend me and keep me in a boozy state even though I was back in Canada. I didn't realize that at ze time, but in hindsight, I see it. If God hadn't delivered me, I would still be there. But He did, and through prayer and his guidance, I have finally found you. I have a wife, children—your cousins—and a family who will accept you with open arms in Canada. I have finally come to restore you to your true family," Remi says.

"Gilda is *my* sister! She's *my* sister!" Goldie says breaking into tears again.

Putting my arms around her, I can't believe how much love I feel for her and how much sadness I feel for both of us.

"You will always be my sister, my true sister no matter what. Nothing will change that," I say holding her close.

"Goldie, you are more than welcome to join us, too. It's up to you. You will be treated as family as well. I would be thrilled to be your uncle," Remi says

"Is Granny going to prison? What is going to happen?" Goldie asks.

"You better believe I'm not going to prison for this made-up pack of lies," Granny says pounding her fists on the table.

"Not from anything I'm going to do. Ze time to try to prosecute any of this is over. With Katrina's millions, I'm sure she has covered up all evidence to support my story. The only retribution that will come from me, Katrina, including anything to do with the US patent, is if you try to keep Gilda, or Goldie if she wishes, from freely coming and being with her family in Canada. Or, if you come after me in any way. This is ze time to forgive. My faith says I am to forgive you. It doesn't feel right to do that, and I am still incredibly angry, but I will follow what it says in ze Bible in Matthew; we must forgive. None of us deserve to be forgiven for everything we have done, yet Jesus forgives us. We must do ze same. *I* must do ze same," Remi says. "I forgive you, Katrina. I will leave the justice you deserve to God."

"No one asked you to forgive me, you self-righteous pig. I don't forgive you. You think you can show up after all these years and ruin the life I've made for my granddaughters. I'm leaving this ridiculous room, and I'll be leaving this island in the morning. Girls, I expect you to be leaving with me," Granny says getting up and moving toward the door. "Come along, Jeeves. Oh, and Jeeves, don't think I've forgotten what you said."

Storming out the door Granny glares at Remi on her way out. Jeeves follows but turns around momentarily to silently mouth the words "It's all true" before going through the door.

I feel like a puddle or a deflated balloon. This is much more than one mind can take in.

"Do you believe me, girls?" Remi asks.

"Everything you are saying answers so many questions I've had through the years. I know Granny is on the shady side, but the fact she could do all that is what really makes my head and my heart hurt," I say. "It's beyond evil."

"She fell for ze love of money more than ze love of people. She became even more ruthless after the accident. Money and getting more money seem to be her motivation for living. Ze Bible says that ze love of money, not money itself, but putting it first place in your life, is ze root of all evil. I'll let you draw your own conclusions," Remi says. "Goldie, I meant what I said. You are family to me, too."

"What if all of this isn't true? I mean, what if…I don't know…you're trying to ease your conscience, because so many people died in the car accident. It could be all made up, it could!" Goldie says in a panicky voice.

"Did you see Jeeves when he left?" I ask. "He was letting us know it was all true. He has been loyal to Granny all these years, and he finally had the courage to tell us the truth."

"I mean Granny supports us. What are we supposed to do, move to Canada, and then do what?" Goldie says looking at Remi.

"I have amassed considerable wealth, Goldie. I will take care of you and Gilda and help you pursue whatever path you want in the US or Canada, whatever you want," Remi says.

"I'm not your relation. I'm nothing to you. And you coming here has only resulted in your attempt to take the most precious thing in the world to me. It will never be the same between Gilda and I now, never! You've ruined that, don't you see? She will always know we aren't twins. And now you both have gotten all religiousy and say God talks to you and I don't know if I want anything to do with that either! I need time for myself. I'm out of here," Goldie says turning toward the door.

"Goldie, we will always be twins in our hearts. Sisters. Always. Why don't you take a minute and then come to my room? We need to talk before tomorrow," I say.

"I don't know if I can be with someone who believes all this. I don't think I do believe it all. Can we really believe someone we've known for several weeks compared to someone we've known our whole lives? I don't know. I don't know what I'm going to do," she says leaving and slamming the door behind her.

"I'm so sorry you had to hear all of this, Gilda. And now you see why I couldn't tell you much before. I had to wait until I could confront Katrina and finally put an end to this whole thing," Remi says. "That's why you've seen people around me that you mistrusted. I've had private investigators on this for years. Once we found out you were here, I had to see if you were happy and okay with your life. Now that I hear you are a child of God's forever family, I'm even more sure I did ze right thing by you, and in ze memory of my dear brother who is not here to speak for himself."

"I have to pray. It's all I can think of doing right now. I'm not going to go with Granny tomorrow. That's one thing I do know. But I'm not sure about Goldie. I'm also not positive I am going to Canada with you...Uncle Remi," I say.

"Oh, how I love to hear those words, 'Uncle Remi.' I understand. If you need money or..."

"Unbeknownst to Granny, I have stashed some of cash that she doesn't know about. I have enough to live on for a while but thank you for the offer. I've always wanted to break away from Granny, but Goldie is so tied to her money, she wouldn't hear of it. Now I have to pray about all this. I'll see you tomorrow. I don't know if Granny is going to make a big scene before she leaves. I wouldn't put it past her..."

"I will be praying, too. God is always in control and none of this is a surprise to Him. He has taken my broken life and worked it together for the good and His Glory as it says in the book of Romans. He will show us ze way forward if we wait on Him," Remi says. "If you need anything, anything, here's my room number. Please call me. We will meet in ze morning to talk more. Bonsoir, my dear niece," Remi says coming over and gently kissing me on the forehead.

A relative! I have a real loving relative unlike I've never had. But do all these good things mean I might lose my sister? Oh, Lord, help!

CHAPTER TWENTY-FIVE

A night of no sleep. A night of crying. A night of prayer and reading in my Bible.

I thought about calling Piper, but remembered she and Cam were on the mainland for a meeting, coming back today. There hasn't been a peep from Goldie, and that is scaring me. I feel like talking to Uncle Remi, but I don't at the same time. Perhaps Goldie needs to sleep, and she is resting. I can't believe she would choose Granny after all she heard, yet she didn't sound convinced when she left. Lord, I simply do not know. All I know is I better be downstairs to see if Granny is leaving right away. There's sure to be a scene, but after what we just went through, nothing will compare to what I saw last night.

I'm choosing a ponytail and my hair up in a baseball cap, jeans, and a sweatshirt. Granny will know my decision right away. One doesn't wear jeans, a ball cap, and a sweatshirt when traveling with Granny.

Granny. She isn't my granny. She is nothing to me. No relative of any kind. So strange. One part of me is happy that someone so evil is not blood related, but the other part feels orphaned. But, I still have Goldie. And Uncle Remi and his family. It will get better.

MICHÈLE OLSON

Here I go. I hope the Academy Awards committee is standing around, because I'm sure I'm about to see the performance of the century.

CHAPTER TWENTY-SIX

Most of the guests aren't up this early. That should make it easier to see if Goldie and Granny are on the porch or the lower level. Maybe they are in the Audubon room or somewhere in the parlor. There's almost an eerie stillness that frightens me.

"I hope I'm not late. I'm here to support you, or to stand back, whatever you need," Uncle Remi says running up to me. "I wanted to beat you downstairs, but you beat me, I think."

"I've been here a little while and hardly anyone is up, but I have not seen Granny, Goldie, or even Jeeves for that matter," I say.

"Maybe everyone is so worn out from ze trauma of yesterday, they are all sleeping in," he says.

"No, if Granny says she's leaving first thing in the morning, she is. Let's go ask the porter if he's dealt with luggage this morning," I say gesturing for Uncle Remi to follow me downstairs near the check in desk.

"Excuse me, sir, did anyone leave yet this morning?" I ask the porter.

"No, not this early. I'm just now getting bags for the first ferry," he says.

I know Granny's luggage. It stands out because it's bright red with big pink flowers. She doesn't do anything subtly.

"No big piece of bright red luggage, unlike most luggage you see coming through here?" I ask.

"Now that you mention it, a piece came down later last night along with a few more pieces, including a pink one, but they aren't here this morning. Huh. That is odd," he says.

"Thank you. I have my answers now," I say.

"What do you think happened?" Uncle Remi asks.

"Simple. Granny has money. She didn't want to wait around for my answer. She already decided she wasn't waiting for me, so she hired a private boat to take her to the mainland. The fact that there was pink luggage mentioned, that would be Goldie. Goldie has gone with her. I can't believe it," I say trying to hold back the tears.

"You are not alone, Gilda. You have me, my family, your forever family as God's child, and good friends like Piper," Uncle Remi says patting my shoulder.

"I know, and I'm grateful, but when you think you've had a twin sister your whole life, losing her is breaking my heart. And as terrible as Granny is, she didn't even wait to see what I was going to say," I say.

"She knew what you were going to say, what any rational person presented with ze facts would have to say in that situation," he says.

"Exactly. How could Goldie go with her? She didn't even give me a chance to talk to her last night or call me. She must have gone to Granny right after she left our dinner. Maybe it's temporary. Maybe she left me a note or something. I'm going to ask at the check-in area," I say heading over to the desk. "Excuse me, I'm Gilda Locks, was anything left for me?"

"Why yes, Miss Locks. Someone left an envelope for you here. Here you go. And while I have you here, well, this is a little delicate to tell you, but your account has been turned off with instructions not to pay for your tab or room anymore. Do you have another way to cover your costs?" she asks.

This is like getting stabbed with a knife.

"Uh, Miss. I am Remi Chapeau. Gilda is my niece. Please transfer all costs associated with Miss Lock's room to my account.," Uncle Remi says.

"No problem, Mr. Chapeau. Yes, I can see that will work perfectly," she says.

Turning away from the desk to Uncle Remi, I am at a loss for words.

"Uncle Remi, really, I have some money set aside. You don't need to…"

"I want to. You need nothing else to worry about. I told you I will take care of you, and I meant it."

"Thank you. I'm too confused to think straight right now. I think I need some time to myself and to read this alone. I know it has to be from Goldie. And I didn't get any sleep last night. Can we meet for dinner tonight at six and talk? I'll be more level-headed then. I might have a greater understanding of what is happening," I say.

"Of course, my sweet girl. Go read your letter, get some rest, and I'll see you for dinner. Just don't let thoughts run away from you. Remember, God will lead and guide you through every next step."

"Thank you," I say.

I know God is with me and now Uncle Remi. But life without my sister, my twin? A blood test may say we're not related, but she is the true sister of my heart. What have you done, Goldie?

CHAPTER TWENTY-SEVEN

I hope no one is there I want to be there, and I want to be alone.

Oh good. It's so early there's no one here. Sitting on this bench in this special little place that feels sacred to me feels right. I'm so glad Piper showed me this labyrinth, the place where Jesus became real to me.

Okay, Gilda. It will be okay. Just open it.

Carefully opening the envelope, I see a five-dollar bill is laying inside. What in the world? Unfolding the letter, I see it is from Goldie. Like the curls on her head, she has the cutest curly way of doing the end of her letters, almost like calligraphy. And she only writes with these special pens she sends away for. Oh, my Goldie.

Dearest Gilda,

This isn't exactly how I wanted you to get the news that I have left, but I think in the long run it is for the best. It's going to save a scene and a flood of tears I don't think I could bear.

And Goldie could never spell. She's heard so much about *Goldie Locks and the Three Bears* her whole life, she doesn't know this type of bare is b-a-r-e. She is one-of-a-kind. So many sweet sister things only I know about her.

I ran into Granny right after I left the dinner room. She was very sweet to me and much more like when we were younger. She even hugged me like a real grandmother! I don't want you to think I'm dumb, and I fell for this. I know in my heart most of what we heard was probably true. But she is my mother's mother. She is my only relative. You have your uncle now, and as kind as he was to me, he is not my uncle.

I feel l must look out for myself and at least see this to the next step. And don't get mad, but Granny did point out that I would now be her only hair.

I know she means heir. Of course, Granny would appeal to Goldie's love of money.

I made her promise that if I didn't like the school, I could quit, and she wouldn't leave me penniless. With your uncle's kind offer to support us, I can use that as an ace up my sleeve when she threatens me about money. That will make all the difference for me in how I deal with her in the future.

So, for the first time, we will be apart for a while. But we do need to learn how to live without each other on a daily basis. That was probably something coming soon anyway. We couldn't stay the Lock sisters locked up in Granny World forever. There were many terrible times but having you as my sister was always the best.

I know you think I'm a narcaci....narci...you know, always thinking about myself, but I'm not. I'm mostly always thinking of how much I love having you for a sister. You're the only person who has truly loved me, and you will always be my sister, my twin sister. No story or circumstances can change that. I hope you feel the same, even after you meet cousins and Remi's big family.

So, now you know I am gone. I do think it saved a big scene with Granny. I hope you agree it's for the best. I will keep an eye on her and if she does anything towards you or your uncle, I will shut it down. You are safe.

Take some time to be with your uncle and family, and when the time is right, we will both know it. We will find each other. Sisters can always find each other. Who knows? Maybe we can be together next spring on Mackinac Island for a true vacation.

I hope I will always live in your heart as your true sister. You are my heart, and I love you forever.

Your sister,

Goldie

P.S. You still need more blush. Take this $5 and get the kind I told you about.

Bursting out laughing, I'm glad no one is around to see my face. I'm a mixture of tears streaming down my face and laughing hilariously. I can tell that even though we are apart right now, Goldie is okay. She is watching out for herself, and she has much more leverage against Granny, now, which will make all the difference in how Granny can try to control her.

I jump a foot as I hear rustling coming from the entrance. Oh darn, someone is going to see me. I better wipe my face and make a dash for it. I don't want to make niceties to some tourists this morning.

CHAPTER TWENTY-EIGHT

"Gilda! Don't jump, it's me!"

Oh, the soothing voice of a friend.

"Piper! What are you doing here so early in the morning, and how did you know I was here? Don't take me wrong, I'm so happy to see you, but you did startle me," I say.

"Remi called me this morning. He said he couldn't say much, that was up to you, but he thought it would be very good if I could find you and give you a hug this morning. He said he saw you walk down the stairs and wasn't sure where you went. I assured him, I'd be happy to supply that hug, and I knew exactly where to find you," Piper says opening her arms.

Hugging her closely for a moment, more tears come, and she lets me sob on her shoulder for a few minutes.

"Here, here is the spare handkerchief I always carry. My friend Sister Mary-Margaret was the friend who taught me to always have a clean hanky for a friend. Very old school I know, but I buy my hankies by the dozen because I love that I can do this for my dear ones," she says handing me a beautiful, embroidered hanky.

"This is too pretty to use! I have tissues…"

"Use it. It somehow always makes the tears better. I don't know how, but it does," she says.

Taking the hanky, I dab the rest of the tears that haven't fallen to water the labyrinth. This place has probably seen many tears.

"Do you want to be alone some more, or do you want to talk?" she asks.

"I want to talk, and I want you to know so many things that you have no idea about."

Watching her eyes widen and her mouth gape as I tell her some background and the tale of the last twenty-four hours, at least I know I'm not crazy. This *is* quite the story. Finally, I read her Goldie's letter.

"Wow! I mean, wow! Kris isn't who he said he was, and well, we know what Katherine is capable of...so no big surprise there. But your granny, your mother, your uncle is Remi...if I saw all this in a movie, I wouldn't even believe it!" Piper says. "Now that you mention it, Cam did say to me later that day we were all together that something was fishy about how Kris...or Vincent I guess, talked about football. He said if the guy could kick the way he said he did, he would be the star of any NFL team. But, oh Gilda. Your sister Goldie. That's the hardest part of all of this."

"It is. But I feel hope from what she said that we will be okay. It will never be quite the same as when we knew we were twins. She now has so much leverage against Granny's evil ideas. My greatest prayer right now is that she will come to know what you told me about; God loves us and has a plan for each of our lives," I say softly. "I wish she would have come to know Jesus while we were here, but she didn't."

"We each still have our own will, but you've planted a seed. Let's pray that people come into her life who can also help her see the truth. God doesn't want anyone to be left out, and that even includes Granny. Our big God can do much more than we even imagine, so let's believe that Granny and Goldie will come to know Him. Cam, Freddy, and I will be praying about it for sure," Piper says.

"Yes, and with Uncle Remi, and his family praying, too... I'm going to believe it's all possible," I say. "I am going to go and meet them I've decided. Then I'll keep praying and see what I'm supposed to do next."

"Good thinking. I'm sure Remi and his family are involved in a good church, but even if they aren't, make sure you find one where you can keep studying God's word and being with other Christians. That's important," Piper says.

"You're right. I will do that. I don't want to be like that story we read in the Bible where the seed falls in the good ground but never gets watered and then dies. I don't want to be *that* seed," I say.

"You are doing all the right things to learn more about being a Christian. I'm so proud of you. Now, let's take a deep breath and say the twenty-third Psalm together. You know the one that starts, The Lord is my Shepherd..." Piper says taking my hands.

"I remember studying it, but I don't have it memorized. You say it and I'll agree in my heart." I say.

"Okay I may paraphrase a word or two, but let's pray knowing God hears every word and everything about this situation. *The Lord is my Shepherd; I have everything I need. He invites me to lie down in green pastures: He leads me beside the still waters. He restores my soul. He leads me in the paths of righteousness for His name's sake. Even if I walk through the valley of the shadow of death, I won't fear evil for He is with me. His rod and staff comfort me. He prepares a table before me in the presence of my enemies, He anoints my head with oil and my cup runs over. Surely goodness and mercy will follow me all the days of my life and I will live with Him forever in His home. Amen.*"

"Amen. I want to get that memorized the way you do. It's very comforting. The part about not fearing evil seems very appropriate after seeing Granny's true colors."

"It is comforting. That's why I memorized it. I need it every day. Here's something I do to help myself, and you may find it helpful. I visualize myself sitting with Jesus and telling him the things that are bothering me. Then I imagine Him answering me, looking at me. It helps me think about the fact He actually is with me and hearing everything we talk about and that He does answer," Piper says.

"I love that. I'm going to try that, too."

"Now, how are you doing? You said you barely slept, and I bet you've hardly eaten. Do you want to walk into town and get some breakfast? I have Freddy minding the store for a few more hours," she says.

"Yes. Now that you mention it, I'm starving. That sounds great. I would like to make one more stop before we eat," I say.

"Sure, where do you need to go?" Piper asks as we get up and move out of the labyrinth and head across the lawn.

"I need to stop at the general market and go to their little make up section," I say half giggling, waving the five-dollar bill from the envelope. "I have a directive from my sister that I need more blush. The next time I see her, and I know I will see her again, I need my makeup to be 'just-right.'"

The End

Dear Reader,

I hope you enjoyed meeting Goldie and Gilda Locks. This is the first time a Mackinac Island story has featured the beauty of Autumn.

Gilda Locks was very honest with her questions about God and life. These are the types of questions we've all had at some point in our own story. Her questions lead her to the ultimate answer. While this story is fiction, there is a very real forever family that awaits each of us. That's what life is all about. Do yourself a favor and read the book of John. The book is also about you!

Please stay in touch for the latest news!

Facebook.com/LakeGirlPublishing

My private Facebook team — Piper's Island Peeps:
    Facebook.com/groups/piperpenn

X formerly Twitter @MoDawnWriter

Instagram.com/lakegirlpublishing

My etsy site featuring cards and Bookmark Betty™ bookmarks:
    www.etsy.com/shop/LakeGirlPublishing

I also do commission artwork in various sizes from small to wall size. If you like my
    art—let's talk!

Sign up for my newsletter: www.lakegirlpublishing.com/connect
    (I love to hear from readers!)

My email: Info@LakeGirlPublishing.com

DEAR READER

My website: www.LakeGirlPublishing.com

My heartfelt thanks,

Michèle

Stories Set on Mackinac Island Filled with Mystery, Mayhem, Mirth, Miracles, and a Splash of Romance !

Ten Things You Can Do to Keep These Stories Going!

1. **Leave a review.** If you liked the books, leave a kind review. Reviews can be brief but never give away plot lines or spoilers. Your encouraging words may be the catalyst that introduces someone else to the story — especially important! From Goodreads to all the places books are sold online, your review matters.
2. **Talk about this book on your social media platforms.** Tell your friends that you enjoyed it. Go to other reader Facebook sites like *Avid Readers of Christian Fiction* and sites that love Mackinac Island. Recommend my books.
3. **Ask your local library to carry the book(s).** In addition, *Being Ethel (In a world that loves Lucy)* is also available in an audiobook, often popular for library borrowing. All the other books are available as eBooks and audiobooks on Amazon.
4. **Contact me to speak at your women's group.** Does your women's group need a speaker? I am a speaker for women's and church groups as well as being an author. www.LakeGirlPublishing.com/speaker
5. **Let me know who you are through my website.** Sign up and get my newsletters.

www.LakeGirlPublishing.com/connect

6. **Use these books as gifts!** Email me if you'd like a sticker for the inside of the book, personalized to someone.
7. **Check out my non-fiction book, *5 Easy Steps to a Happy Birthday!*** No adult should ever have a ho-hum birthday ever again.

10 THINGS YOU CAN DO

8. **Pray for me!** I appreciate your prayers! My books have a message of hope and faith, and my desire is to get them to as many people as possible.
9. **Interact with me on social media.** Follow my Facebook.com/LakeGirlPublishing page and my private team's Facebook page, Piper's Island Peeps, for those who are very enthusiastic about my books.
10. **Leave a review!** (No, that's not a typo, it's so important it gets to be on here twice!)

Want a list of questions for your book club to read one (or all) of my books? Send me an email. I'm happy to provide book club questions.

I love to hear from readers! info@lakegirlpublishing.com
My website: www.LakeGirlPublishing.com

Thank you for being a part of my team:
Piper Penn's Island Peeps!

READ THEM IN ORDER, OR AS STAND-ALONES

This is the sixth book in my Mackinac Island Story series. The book stands on its own as a single offering; however, you will find it an even richer story if you read the first book in the series, *Being Ethel (In a world that loves Lucy)*, where we meet Piper Penn for the first time. It's set in 1979. The next book in the series is *Being Dorothy (In a world longing for home)* where Piper Penn meets a mysterious couple on the porch of the Grand Hotel, set in 1980. But are they who they seem to be? It's a story with a James Bond flair. The third book *Being Alice (In a world lost in the looking glass)* is set in 1981. A young musical genius has scars on her face that don't compare to the scars in her heart. Anyone who has ever loved a singer/songwriter and music will enjoy this story. The fourth book, set in 1982, is *Being Wendy (In a world afraid to grow up)*. A novel with a nod to Peter Pan, this story follows Wendy T. Bell, a famous author who is sure someone at her fiftieth birthday party is trying to end her career, or worse! She escapes to Mackinac Island and meets Pan Feters. Mysterious things keep happening and they don't stop! The fifth book in the series is *Being Nancy (In a world lost in mystery)* where you will find yourself at a Nancy Drew Convention at Grand Hotel in 1983. Nancy Benson enlists the island favorites in a committee

READ THEM IN ORDER, OR AS STAND-ALONES

to help pull this off, but when a first edition of *The Mystery at Lilac Inn* goes missing everyone involved looks guilty and can be in real trouble. Anyone who grew up loving Nancy Drew will adore the almost thirty references to the girl sleuth, plus the mayhem and mirth in this story.

How to help spread the news of these stories!

■ Leave a review at all the big book sites. As an author, let me assure you this is super important! It helps me be found by other readers in the mass world of books.

■ Give these books as gifts! Share the eBook and/or paperback versions with friends and family for birthdays and "just because." Fuel Faith with Fiction™ and join us as a #papermissionary!

■ Join me on social media and share my posts. All contacts are listed in this book.

Time to dive into this treasure. I can't wait for you to meet Goldie and Gilda Locks.

Blessings,

Michèle

Meet Michèle Olson

Michèle Olson had an over forty-five-year career in advertising and marketing as a writer in all mediums, with an emphasis on health writing before she retired to Lake Girl Publishing. She also enjoys a professional voice career including time as a DJ (yes, even when they still played records!) and continues to voice local to national commercials and voice projects.

It has always been her dream to segue into fiction and *Being Ethel (In a world that loves Lucy)* was her first in a series based on Mackinac Island — a tiny island in the Straits of Mackinac that connects the Upper and Lower Peninsula of Michigan A visitor there, along with her husband, for over thirty years, loves to tell people about this unique place with no cars and plenty of fudge!

She is thrilled to share *Being Ethel (In a world that loves Lucy), Being Dorothy (In a world longing for home), Being Alice (In a world lost in the looking glass), Being Wendy (In a world afraid to grow up), Being Nancy (In a world lost in mystery),* and this new offering: *Being Goldie (In a "just-right" world).*

A mom, a mother-in-love, and a "Gee Gee" (G as in good), Michèle resides with her husband in the shadow of Lambeau Field, where life around football abounds. She cherishes her faith and family above all and is delighted to take you on another trip to Mackinac Island, a place that has brought her so much respite and joy. You can also see her other love: art and doodling! See her projects on her website and Etsy site where you can find quirky and fun bookmarks under her Bookmark Betty™ line of bookmarks and cards. www.etsy.com/shop/LakeGirlPublishing

She loves connecting, so reach back through all the social media links provided.

Stay connected for more stories from Michèle Olson. www.LakeGirlPublishing.com/connect

Ten places to explore if you go to Mackinac Island! (There are many more, too!)

1. **Little Stone Church. (Featured in this novel!)** A registered Michigan historic site, The Little Stone Church is actually called The Union Congregational Church. It was formed in 1899 and built of local field stone in 1904 in an eclectic Gothic style. The interior gleaming woodwork and deep-set stained-glass windows are virtually unchanged and represent the history of Mackinac Island. The church still holds Sunday services and remains open primarily in the summer hours.
2. **Arch Rock.** This is a natural rock bridge that sits 149 feet above the Straits of Mackinac as if it's suspended in midair! You can walk there, or you can stop as part of a carriage tour. It's fun to see from below or up close.
3. **Fort Mackinac.** Known to be the oldest building in Michigan, you can see history come alive and imagine yourself living in a military outpost. It's the fortress on a bluff you see as you come into the harbor. Listen at certain times of the day — the cannon does work!
4. **St. Anne's Catholic Church.** This beautiful church is worth seeing, including the stained-glass windows. Of course, if you're like me, you imagine Sister Mary Margaret —from *Being Ethel (In a world that loves Lucy)*—sitting in a pew waiting to have a conversation with you.
5. ***Somewhere in Time,*** the wonderful movie filmed on the island in 1979 and part of *Being Ethel (In a world that loves Lucy)*, my first novel in this series, boasts multiple island treasure stops. Seek out the "Is it you?" spot with a plaque commemorating the line

and, of course, the famed gazebo. Relocated from its original place in the movie, anyone on the island can tell you where to find it!

6. **Fort Holmes**. Do you like to hike? Go to this highest point on the island, even higher up than Fort Mackinac. Originally named Fort George, it was renamed when the Americans returned to the fort in 1815. In 2015, it was reconstructed for visitors to learn more about its amazing history.
7. **Round Island Lighthouse.** You'll pass this beautiful lighthouse as you ferry in and away from the island. Not a spot for visitors, as much as sightseers, you'll find yourself looking for it whenever you are near the shores of the island. It, too, has a pivotal scene in *Somewhere in Time*. Besides, don't you just love lighthouses?
8. **Sugar Loaf.** It's an adventurous hike or bike ride to make it to this tall geological formation but worth it. How many times have you seen a limestone stack on an island? You see my point!
9. **The Grand Hotel**. Of course! Either go for a stay or pay the minimal fee and walk around for a day. Be sure to sit on that famous porch on a white wicker rocking chair and imagine you are having a conversation with Piper Penn!
10. **The Island Bookstore.** Located inside The Lilac Tree entrance on Main St., this wonderful bookstore has been bringing the best in books to island visitors for decades! You can get a Mackinac Island favorite or browse the wide variety of books available. Stop in and take a picture of my books! **Send me a pic of you there with my book(s), and I'll send you a wonderful treat in the mail!**

NON-FICTION BY MICHÈLE OLSON

Non-fiction by Michèle Olson

5 Easy Steps to a Happy Birthday!
A practical, funny guide to a Happy Birthday every single year!

When was the last time, as an adult, you had a glorious, fun-filled, satisfying, memorable Happy Birthday? If that's not your norm, it's time for a change! Whether circumstances, apathy, or disappointment have pushed you into a world of ho-hum birthdays, this is your chance to recover the bliss of a well-celebrated birthday—on your terms.

Filled with practical suggestions, get ready for an outrageously gratifying, joyous, and "dream come true" birthday—every year. Everyone should have a Happy Birthday, every single year! Get ready to celebrate! This is a great gift and stocking stuffer.

Paperback, wherever books are sold, including Amazon.
eBooks and audiobooks, on Amazon.

FREEBIES AND MORE FUN!

Would you like a personalized signed sticker for your book?

Simply email me. I'll let you know how to get one when you send a Self-Addressed Stamped Envelope. Also, it's a great gift idea!

Are you going to Mackinac Island? Please take some pictures of my book on the island at various places and in The Island Bookstore! Send me some pics of you and fun book pics. I'll send you a special prize!

info@lakegirlpublishing.com

Email me! info@lakegirlpublishing.com
 Check out my art shops: Etsy featuring the bookmarks and cards of my Bookmark Betty™ line.
 https://www.etsy.com/shop/LakeGirlPublishing

Fine Art America:
 https://www.fineartamerica.con/profiles/2-michele-olson

Need a speaker for your conference? Check out my speaker page at:
 www.LakeGirlPublishing.com/speaker

Keynote and breakout session speaker with Doodling and Sketchnote sessions including teaching others to doodle with joy!

Looking for some of the Bible verses talked about in *Being Goldie (In a "just-right" world)* ?

The Message Bible is one of my favorite Bible versions. It was not yet written at the time of this story, but I thought you would enjoy seeing some of the verses in this book as they are expressed in *The Message*. Blessings!

John 3:16-18 *This is how much God loved the world: He gave his Son, his one and only Son. And this is why: so that no one need be destroyed; by believing in him, anyone can have a whole and lasting life. God didn't go to all the trouble of sending his Son merely to point an accusing finger, telling the world how bad it was. He came to help, to put the world right again. Anyone who trusts in him is acquitted; anyone who refuses to trust him has long since been under the death sentence without knowing it. And why? Because of that person's failure to believe in the one-of-a-kind Son of God when introduced to him.*

Luke 10:41-42 *The Master said, "Martha, dear Martha, you're fussing far too much and getting yourself worked up over nothing. One thing only is essential, and Mary has chosen it—it's the main course, and won't be taken from her."*

The Story of Mary and Martha: Luke 10:38-42

Matthew 6:30-33 *"If God gives such attention to the appearance of wildflowers—most of which are never even seen—don't you think he'll attend to you, take pride in you, do his best for you? What I'm trying to do here is to get you to relax, to not be so preoccupied with getting, so you can respond to God's giving. People who don't know God and the way he works fuss over these things, but you know both God and how he works. Steep your life in God-reality, God-initiative, God-provisions. Don't worry about missing out. You'll find all your everyday human concerns will be met.*

Luke 15:8-10 *"Or imagine a woman who has ten coins and loses one. Won't she light a lamp and scour the house, looking in every nook and cranny until she finds it? And when she finds it you can be sure she'll call her friends and neighbors: 'Celebrate with me! I found my lost coin!' Count on it—that's the kind of party God's angels throw every time one lost soul turns to God."*

Psalm 23 *God, my shepherd!*
I don't need a thing.
You have bedded me down in lush meadows,
you find me quiet pools to drink from.
True to your word,
you let me catch my breath
and send me in the right direction.
Even when the way goes through
Death Valley,
I'm not afraid
when you walk at my side.
Your trusty shepherd's crook
makes me feel secure.

You serve me a six-course dinner
right in front of my enemies.
You revive my drooping head;
my cup brims with blessing.
Your beauty and love chase after me
every day of my life.
I'm back home in the house of God
for the rest of my life.

Hey, have you read the Bible for yourself?
The greatest mystery of endless love awaits you!

www.ingramcontent.com/pod-product-compliance
Lightning Source LLC
LaVergne TN
LVHW040055080526
838202LV00045B/3652